I0606839

Isaac P. Bielby

Sheriffs of Oneida County

Isaac P. Bielby

Sheriffs of Oneida County

ISBN/EAN: 9783743335271

Manufactured in Europe, USA, Canada, Australia, Japa

Cover: Foto ©Raphael Reischuk / pixelio.de

Manufactured and distributed by brebook publishing software
(www.brebook.com)

Isaac P. Bielby

Sheriffs of Oneida County

SHERIFFS

—OF—

NEIDA COUNTY,

—BY—

ISAAC P. BIELBY.

1890.

SHERIFFS

—OF—

NEIDA COUNTY,

—BY—

ISAAC P. BIELBY.

1890.

UTICA, N. Y.:

THE office of Sheriff has descended to us from bygone days. Some historians with great show of probable truth, have placed its origin in the proconsel of the ancient Romans; others have endeavored to trace it to corresponding positions under patriarchs, emperors and kings. But whatever may be the fact, it is the same now as it was a thousand years ago in the reign of Alfred the Great. He brought from out the chaos of Anglian governmental machinery, a tangible division of his Kingdom into Sceyres or Earldoms, now called counties or shires. The government of these shires was entrusted to an Earl or Comes. The Shire Keeper was the same as our Sheriff. He was appointed and ordained by the King as Keeper of the Peace and Governor of the Shire. His power was very great; he executed the King's commands and ruled with authority of his own. In many cases he was an arbitary tyrant, having the discretionary powers of Judge, Jury and Executioner. In due time came the Magna Charter of John, an enactment memorable for its construction and frequent violation. It was constantly and continually being confirmed and reconfirmed until in 1216, Henry III, then a minor, had it revised and re enacted. It was duly confirmed by the Earl of Pembroke and Papal Nuncio. When the King attained his majority it was again reconfirmed in the form in which it appears on our law books. This act modifies the judicial authority. The statute of Edward I, gave the people the right to elect their own Sheriffs, but the officers used their power to secure a re-election and so abused their trust, that the people asked that the law be repealed. Edward II caused the constitution to be so amended as to give the nominating power to the Judges of the courts. No person was allowed to take the appointment unless he had sufficient land and property to answer to the King and the people During the following reign it was enacted that no person should hold the office more than one year. Under Richard III it was declared that no man who had served should be chosen again within three years. This was enforced by Henry VI by an act to secure its observance. Large penalties were imposed for any violation, one-half going to the King and the remainder to the informer. By another act in the same reign, Sheriffs were allowed to take bail and appoint constables or bailiffs to attend the courts in their shires. At this time, the Sheriff received no salary, or fees. The office was honorary and soon became onerous and burdensome. He was not a creature of the crown, but of the Courts. Later he was again made the King's representative in the county and his power enlarged. The bailiffs or constables were under him as keepers of the town. Ten families of freeholders constituted a town or tithing, ten of these towns constituted a hundred, which was placed under the government of a high constable or bailiff, who, in ancient days, presided in the hundreds court. An indefinite number of the hundreds made up a shire or county. Under his combined judicial and executive authority, the Sheriff could both arrest and try offenders. He stood under the commission of the King, the arbitrary ruler of the shire. At his command the people must obey under the penalty of fine and imprisonment.

By statute of Henry IV if any riot or unlawful assembly or rout of people was made against the law within the Kingdom, whether in the presence of some justice or otherwise, the justices of the peace not less than two in number, and three as a quorum, and the Sheriff or Under Sheriff of the county, were enjoined to come with the power of the county and arrest them. They were also required to make a record of all that was done and in their discretion the offenders could be convicted. The power of the county or possee comitatus was regulated by statute of Henry VI by which it was enacted that the Kings' liege people, except women, infants under fifteen years, persons decrepit and clergymen, being sufficient to travel, shall be assistants to the justice upon reasonable warning to ride with them in aid to resist riots and punish the offenders. They were also authorized to take with them such weapons as should be neccesay to overcome and secure their prisoners. Beating, wounding and even killing was justified under this law. The sheriff must be a man of 21 years, fair education, sound mind and good judgment This is the way the law stood in England in the colonial days of American settlement.

COLONIAL DAYS.

In the early colonial days of the Empire State the Dutch "West India Company" had control of the laws. Under their charter the old Dutch patroon system prevailed. They had by-laws and ordinances of their own. The powers of the Patroon were strictly defined by these laws in New Amsterdam. They made him the representative of the Governor and most influential officer in the city. His powers were even greater than under the English system. When the city and State fell into the hands of the Britons the laws of England went into effect. This was about the year 1665 Alfred Anthony being the first Sheriff. In this case the people were allowed to nominate, but afterwards the Sheriffs were appointed by the Governor. This continued up to the time of the revolution. After the independence of the States was declared and the constitution of 1777 adopted, they were appointed for one year. The first one appointed for the territory including Oneida county, was William Colbrath. He was Sheriff of Herkimer county when Oneida county was organized in 1798. The Clerk of Herkimer county at that time was Jonas Platt who resided at Whitestown in what is now the village of Whitesboro, Oneida county. This probably accounts for the fact that the old records of deeds and mortgages recorded in Herkimer county from its organization in 1791 to 1798 are in Oneida County Clerk's office. It was fortunate they were left here as the Herkimer County Clerk's office was destroyed by fire in 1804. There are very valuable records in all counties west of Schenectady, in matters pertaining to especially soldiers' rights.

ONEIDA COUNTY.

Oneida county was organized in 1798. At that time there were only three sessions of the County Court or Court of Common Pleas and General Sessions held within its limits. The circuit of the Supreme Court and Court of Oyer and Terminer was left to the discretion of the Judges of those courts. A court house and jail were to be built within a mile of Fort Schuyler, otherwise known as Fort Stanwix, at Rome. The first court of record was the Herkimer Common Pleas and General Sessions, held at Whitestown in the meeting house. The next was held at New Hartford in a barn. At this time William Colbrath was Sheriff. There were six indictments found for assault and battery, at these courts, but little other business was done. Thus began the judicial history of Oneida county and its Sheriffs. After this all courts were held alternately at Whitestown and Rome. The first circuit of the Supreme Court and Court of Oyer and Terminer was held at the school house near Fort Stanwix, June 5, 1798. At this court the Hon. James Kent presided with the County Judge and Justices for the session.

THE FIRST MURDER TRIAL.

At this term of court occurred the trial of Sylvia Wood, alias Brown, for murder. Sylvia was charged with shooting her husband while intoxicated, on their return from the general election held at the village of New Hartford. They lived southwest of the village near Augusta. As I write there lies before me a phamplet giving the proceedings of this unnatural case. It was published at the time by the Whitestown Gazette. From this sketch of her life I learn that Sylvia was an unfortunate and wayward woman. The vice of intemperance had wrecked and ruined her, and she was now almost friendless and alone. She was convicted and committed to Herkimer county jail to await her sentence. After sentence she was remanded to jail for execution. On the morning fixed for the hanging she was found dead in her cell. She had hanged herself to evade the death penalty. Her body was cut down and given to the surgeons to further the development of medical science. Thus the gallows was cheated, but rum and surgery had its victim. Before her death poor Sylvia called down the vengeance of heaven upon her destroyers and the doctors who should mutilate her body. This so annoyed the surgeon at New Hartford, who did the cutting, that it became one of the unhappy recollections of his life. It is unpleasant to recall these lessons of intemperance in the early history of Oneida county. This was the most important event in the term of Sheriff Colbrath.

ELIZUR MOSELEY.

January 1, 1799. Elizur Moseley was appointed by the Governor to take the place of Sheriff Colbrath. He at once qualified and entered upon the discharge of his official duties. His term was an uneventful one, nothing occurring outside of his ordinary official business to attract public attention. The courts met and adjourned, after trying a few cases, principally for assault and battery. Mosley was a resident of Whitestown and a noble, public spirited citizen. There are many things in the files of the old *Gazette* that commend him for his generosity and the faithful performance of his duty.

CHARLES C. BRODHEAD.

In 1800 Charles C. Brodhead, of Whitesboro, was commissioned by Governor Jay under the amended constitution to serve three years. After entering upon the discharge of his duties he removed to Utica and became prominent in its busines circles. He was one of the great men among the early settlers. The records on file in all the offices of the different counties attest his scholarship and accuracy as a surveyor. He belonged to a family of illustrious names. David Brodhead grandfather of the Sheriff, was commissioned a royal superintendent of Indian affairs by the King of England. His father, Charles Broadhead, was an officer in the British army. He was with General Broadock at the time of his memorable defeat by the French and Indians in ambuscade. During the revolutionary war he favored the colonies, but refused to violate the oath he had taken on entering the service of the British Government. His brothers all served with distinction under Washington, and in the House of Congress. The subject of our sketch served in the Surveyor-General's office of the State and made the preliminary surveys for the Erie canal. At the time of his appointment he was regarded as a leader among men. His term as Sheriff was an eventful one and would have baffled the genius and skill of a man of less ability. Intemperance did a fearful work among the Indians and many riots occurred. But Brodhead's experience with them and knowledge of their language, gave him an influence and power that few other men possessed. At the Court of Oyer and Terminer held at the school house near Fort Stanwix, June 21, 1801, George Peters, a Montauk Indian, was tried for murder and was convicted. George killed his wife in a fit of anger while intoxicated, Feburary 24, 1800, near the village of Rome. He was executed by Sheriff Brodhead on the hills west of Whitesboro, August 28, 1801. This was the first legal execution in Oneida county. Crime was now rapidly increasing and it became necessary to at once complete the jail at Whitesboro. The records of the General sessions held at Rome in 1802, give his report of its completion. He now turned his attention towards enforcing the

law against selling liquor to Indians. At the General Session in May, 1803, several indictments were found. The most notorious offender was Stephen Page, who was convicted and fined $20 penalty and $10 costs. Other cases were disposed of in a similar way. Brodhead was one of the best Sheriffs in the Empire State.

JAMES S. KIPP.

The general election in 1803 was very spirited and exciting. The contest between Thomas Jefferson, Democrat, and Alexander Hamilton, Federalist, for President of the United States, was something like the contests of more modern times. George Clinton was elected Governor of the State of NewYork on the ticket with Jefferson. Oneida county had been strongly Federal, but the loss of territory in the St. Lawrence region made it very close. A great Democratic celebration was now held at Whitesboro, Oneida county. Prominent among those present was the young Democratic leader, James S. Kipp. Governor Clinton admired his ability and political promise and duly made him Sheriff of the county for the ensuing three years. Mr. Kipp was a resident of Utica and one of its leading citizens. He owned at this time a large portion of the land covered by the Second, Third and Eleventh Wards. He commenced in Utica as a business man, but soon became ambitious to shine in other spheres. His first public office seems to have been in a military capacity as inspector of militia, with the rank of Major. His next, that of Sheriff, which he held by repeated appointment for nine years. He was one of the first Board of Directors of the Utica Bank, and in 1812, a Presidential electors. His first residence was on Main street, but he afterwards built an elegant mansion on the westerly side of Broadway. It was surrounded by handsome parks and beautiful parade grounds for military reviews. These were impaired and finally rendered useless by the construction of the Erie canal. He was truly a representative man of the county and the State. Generous almost to a fault, the impress of his noble character shines forth in almost every work of benevolence, education and Christian advancement. As a Christian gentleman he was loved and honored by all who knew him. One of the places nearest to his heart was Hamilton College. He was one of its charter trustees and gloried in its work of culture, learning and refinement. During his three terms as Sheriff, many sad and trying things occurred to test his kind and benevolent spirit. Among them was the killing of Nathan Allen while hunting, near Augusta. The murderer was a drunken, revengeful Indian. Another was the great Indian riot at Oriskany in which several Indians were killed. But the saddest of all was the Halleck tragedy at Westmoreland. Betsey Halleck, who was once a kind and indulgent mother, in a fit of insanity slew her four daughters and then took her own life. Before performing this awful deed she prepared shrouds for each and neatly laid them away for her victims. The real cause of her trouble remains a mystery, but those who knew her best thought it a religious delusion. She sought to remove herself and children from the sorrow and troubles of a cold and selfish world. The great trouble in Kipp's first term was caused by illegal sale of liquor. The law was now such that Sheriffs were appointed for one year or during the pleasure of the Governor.

BENAJAH MERRILL.

On the staff of Sheriff Kipp was Benajah Merrill, of New Hartford. He was a good auctioneer and a profitable man in the office. When the State administration changed in 1807, he was appointed Sheriff and served one year. He then yielded the office to Kipp. Kipp now again served two years. Merrill had removed to Utica and resided on Hotel street. In 1810 he was again appointed Sheriff and served one year and then agrin yielded to Kipp. Nothing of any great moment seems to have transpired while Merrill was Sheriff. He was a very stirring and earnest man in business but not as successful as he was deserving. He was an adroit politician and popular with the people. Kipp now served until 1815—four years. This is what was then known in the Sheriff's office as the war period. There were several Indian riots and the great military riot under General Oliver Collins. During the war of 1812 Utica was a great central camping ground.

THE GREAT COURT MARTIAL.

When the militia were summoned to the front in the war of 1812, many refused to go, some from fear and others from conviction of what they thought right. Many others deserted and ran away from their commands at Sackett's Harbor. After the excitement was over General Collins ordered a general court martial at Utica. A fearful riot occurred and the power of the county was required to prevent serious disorder and bloodshed. This brought the Sheriff in charge as the Chief Executive officer of the county. Finally the court was organized and conducted at the New England House kept by Major John Bellinger. The prisoners were duly tried and convicted. The sentences varied according to the enormity of the offense. When the judgment was about to be carried into effect, another large crowd assembled and offered resistence. The loyal element of the military was now called out and General Collins, who was in command, ordered them to load and if necessary fire. The mob seeing that the Sheriff and General meant business gave way and dispersed. The culprits were then drummed out of town under guard as far as Deerfield Corners. While the United States Arsenal was being built by the Government at Rome, several similar disturbances broke out calling for prompt and decisive action on the part of the Sheriff. Kipp being both a military man and model officer, was always equal to the task, and great responsibility of the Sheriff's office.

APOLLOS COOPER.

Apollos Cooper, another of Utica's pioneers and most distinguished citizens, was appointed to succeed James S. Kipp in 1815. He was a carpenter, designer and architect. His residence was on Whitesboro street. The substantial Mohawk river bridge was the work of his skill, also the plans for Hamilton Academy, now Hamilton College. For several terms he represented the county in the Legislature, and was also one of its Judges. Having located in the county in his younger days he secured a large acquaintance and faithful following. If there were any differences in the community he was sought as an honest and fearless arbiter. Self-reliant and outspoken he was positive in his convictions and fearless in the discharge of every duty. He was in all things a Christian gentleman and an honorable, upright, citizen. Educated in public life he was well qualified for the office and dignity of Sheriff. He served four years. The first capital crime calling for investigation was that of John Parkman, killed at Westmoreland. The case required much skill and care. Parkman was shot while lying in bed with a sick child. He had for some time kept a dog that was disliked in the community and many had threatened to kill him. On the night of the murder the dog was heard to bark about the time Parkman was hit. The facts developed a case against one John Smith, who shot at the dog and killed its master. Smith was convicted of manslaughter and sent to State Prison for a term of three years. This case was hardly disposed of when a row occurred at a general training held at Hampton between a number of drunken militiamen, and a young man by the name of Judson was shot and mortally wounded. Then followed the murder of Joseph Tuhi by John Tuhi. They were brothers and had been to a general training at Clinton, where they became intoxicated and quarrelled over a sum of money. In the melee John struck Joseph with an ax and killed him outright. This was May 17, 1817. He was indicted, tried and convicted and sentenced to be hanged July 25, of the same year. At the appointed time and place, at the head of John street, and perhaps in what is now Rutger Place he was duly executed. He was pinioned and prepared by Under Sheriff John B. Pease, the Sheriff sitting upon his horse near by in full military dress. When the services had concluded the Sheriff rode up to the scaffold and drew his broad sword, severing the rope that held the trap and John Tuhi was swung into eternity. There was a motley, drunken crowd present but no serious disturbance occurred. Then came the mysterious drowning of William Lord at Fish Creek while intoxicated. Many mysterious drownings have taken place at this same place from which it derives the name Rum Hole. Several have been indicted for these offenses. These were terrible years of crime and public disturbances.

BURNING OF THE ROME JAIL.

One of the most revolting disasters in the history of the county, was the burning of the Rome Jail. John Harris, John Denney, James O'Brien, David Linus and Roswell T. Pratt were indicted for murder and arson by reason of their efforts to destroy this place of criminal restraint. They were confined there as prisoners, and on the night of the 19th of August, 1817, set fire to the building They succeeded in effecting their own escape, but an old man named Elisha Green was suffocated and burned to ashes. There were a large number of other prisoners badly injured and taken out for dead. The culprits were at once captured by the Sheriff and his officers and indicted, tried and convicted of murder in the first degree. They were duly sentenced to be hanged on the second Friday of February, 1818. The gallows was erected and all things prepared for the execution. When the day arrived, upon the scaffold stood the Sheriff and the condemned prisoners. They were pinioned and their shrouds and their coffins awaited them. A large concourse of people stood as eager, anxiously awaiting witnesses. The first man was approaching the instrument of death. A painful silence prevailed among the almost breathless, surging crowd below, when a messenger from the Governor appeared upon the stage and read a reprieve staying the execution and changing the sentence to imprisonment for life. He gave as a reason for his action newly discovered evidence showing that Green took part in the burning and was suffocated while engaged in the crime. Denney and Linus were Oneida Indians, confined for assault and larceny while intoxicated. Thus ended one of the most important events in the criminal history of Oneida county.

JOHN B. PEASE.

The efficient Under Sheriff, John B. Pease, succeeded Apollos Cooper in 1819, and served two years. He continued to conduct the office in the same manner as his predecessors. Perhaps no man then living had a more thorough knowledge of the duties of the office. He was a man of fine presence, good ability and very popular with the people. For years he was a resident of Whitestown. The action of the Governor in commuting the sentences of the Rome jail fire bugs had a bad effect on the criminal classes. Minor crimes greatly increased and juries became very cautious in convicting in the higer degrees. John, or Nathan Paul and Maria Bushnell were indicted for murder but convicted of manslaughter. A great riot occurred at Utica at a general celebration in Pease's first year, but was finally quelled by the posse from the Sheriff's office. The cause of the disturbance was too many Indians and too much whisky. In 1820 a grand reception and banquet was given in Utica to General La Fayette, who honored the county with his presence. The Sheriff and his staff figured very prominently in the proceedings on this occasion. The celebration was one of the most successful ever held in Central New York.

JOHN E. HINMAN.

John E. Hinman, of Utica, became the next Sheriff of the county. He was an old and honored citizen, having come to Utica with his father from Little Falls in 1797. His military experience through the various grades to Colonel of the 134th Regiment of New York State Militia and as Deputy Sheriff made him a very competent man for the office. He assumed the duties of Sheriff in February, 1821. The accounts given of his conduct in courts show that he was very dignified in office and popular with the people. He served under his appointment until the office became elective, and in November, 1822, was elected by an overwhelming majority to serve three years more. Affable in manner, shrewd in business, ambitious and kindhearted, he soon became one of the great political leaders of his time. In 1849 he was defeated for State Senator and in 1850 elected Mayor of Utica, and by successive elections held the office three years. It will be remembered that this was during the time of the great fires and riots among rival companies. A man of less ability and experience would have shrunk from the task and avoided the great responsibility. With the Mayoralty ended his political career. There were two murder trials while he was Sheriff but they resulted in convictions for manslaughter only. They were the sons of Francis Aaron and Peter B. Pringle. In November, 1823, the people were shocked by the great Indian disturbances near the Reservation and the wounding of several of their number. The cause was land trespass and fire water. These were hardly quieted by the Sheriff when occurred the more shocking disturbance at Clinton.

RIOT AT HAMILTON COLLEGE.

On the heghts of a beautiful sloping rise of ground, twelve miles southwest of Utica, stands Hamilton College. It has been the soene of many disputes and disturbances among teachers and scholars, but the most astounding one of all was the riot of 1823. There was a tutor in the school who had made himself obnoxious to many of the students and they were bound to drive him out. While the offensive teacher was quietly sleeping in his room one night, they loaded, plugged and sanded a cannon and fired it in a hall near his door. The result was that it nearly ruined part of the building and tore in tatters the clothing and bed of the tutor. His escape from instant death was almost miraculous. The evidence was taken by the proper authorities and the Sheriff and his clerk,but the matter was finally allowed to rest through the influence of the college authorities. May 9, of the following year, occurred the killing of David Freeman by Irod Morse. Both had been hunting, Morse carrying a gun and Freeman a bottle of whisky. Freeman was only a boy about 17 years of age. Morse was a drunken brute and for some unknown cause shot and killed the boy in a fit of anger. He was indicted for murder in the first degree and promptly tried and convicted. The sentence fixed the hanging for December 24, 1824. His sentence was finally commuted to imprisonment for life. Drunkenness in this case was made an excuse for crime. Hinman was a model Sheriff and successful politician, being the recognized leader of the Democracy in the county.

DAVID PIERSON.

The Sheriff's office seems to have been a great political machine from its origin more than a thousand years ago. Thus it was that Deputy David Pierson was elected to succeed Hinman in the fall of 1825, and thus it has been many times ever since. Pierson, like Hinman, was a politician, shrewd and sagacious. Utica was his headquarters. His term opened in 1826, with the indictment, trial and conviction of Cata John and John Church for murder. Like the rest of the murderers of the times they were reprieved and finally committed for manslaughter. In 1827 the Sheriff broke up a gang of counterfeiters in Utica. Among them were Richard Mark, Peter De Long, John Prince and David De Long. These were all tried and convicted. It will be remembered that we only had State banks in those days. Then came the Utica riots and the indictment and trial of two of its most prominent citizens.

It is amusing to study the old criminal records in the County Clerk's Office and find the names of so many illustrious men who have in their younger days been in the custody of the law. I shall only mention those cases where they are prominent and recognized as such in the record. The misdemeanor calendar in the Court of Sessions was very large. The most exciting case was the jail breaking by Charles Metcalf at Utica. Pierson had a very quiet term.

January 1, 1829, John E. Hinman again entered upon the duties of Sheriff for a term of three more years. He was now very wealthy and his wife had a large fortune of her own. He seemed to like office and the fascination of political life The Loomis gang in Sangerfield had now commenced their depredations, and Hinman was determined to break them up if possible. Several indictments were found for assaults and grand larceny. At almost every court for years they figured conspicuously. Complaints were made against them for horse stealing, riot, murderous assaults and unlawfully assembly. Abram Newbury, John C. Drummond, Isaac Harrington, Every Hilland and Lyman Blake were tried and convicted. Then occurred the fearful riot in Westmoreland, for which Grant Adams, Israel S. Adams, John Solets, Anson Pratt and Lelley Hutchinson were indicted and tried. The Sheriff then turned his attention to another gang of counterfeiters at Utica, and soon had in custody John Drew, the leader of the gang. He was convicted and imprisoned. A gambling hell at Utica was also broken up and William Howard, the proprietor, was convicted and punished for the offense. It must be remembered that the Sheriff, Under Sheriff and a few deputies did most of the business in those days. Hinman was so interested in all the industrial enterprises of the city that he took a great pride in enforcing the law.

SAMUEL M. MOTT.

Samuel M. Mott was the next Sheriff of the county for three years. He was at the time of election a popular politician. There doesn't seem to have been much done by him outside of the ordinary routine of business. His term was the beginning of the strife for the office to make money out of it. The population of the county had increased so fast that it now became a good paying office—probably worth from $5,000 to $8,000 per year. There were several disturbances along the line of the canal. Harmon Carpenter, Harmon Carpenter, Jr., Jonathan Whaley, Professor Whaley were arrested, tried and convicted of unlawful assembly. John Griffiths and James Peek were indicted and tried for murder. Also Hugh Rooney. Mott was more of a business man than executive officer.

Erastus Willard, a Vernon farmer, succeeded Mott. He was an old time Whig and bright political manager. His son, a lawyer of Utica, acted as Under Sheriff and the two did all the Sheriff's business in the county. The old members of the bar say they both made themselves comfortably rich. Their plans were well laid and fearlessly executed. They first centered their fire on the Loomis gang. Most of them were indicted, tried and convicted, George Washington Loomis being among the number. The courts commenced their judicial decisions by imposing a fine of $50 and costs. Of course the penalty went to the county and costs to the Sheriff. It was a good job however

and well managed. He then made a raid on a gang of young counterfeiters on Paris Hill. It was composed of some of the most promising young men of the county. They were out of the best families, well educated and discreet. Their downfall was greatly due to the lawlessness by which they were surrounded. The Loomis gang were their near neighbors. Great diligence and prudence had to be used in finding out their operations. They were finally caught, indicted and convicted. Hiram W. Meeker, Daniel Head, Oran Head and George Brown were all sent to States Prison for the offense. These trials were among the most celebrated ever had in the county, eminent counsel being engaged on both sides. Great regret was universally expressed that such talented young men should be classed as criminals. But the condition of things in society demanded the severest punishment. In 1835 came the great slavery agitation. The first convention was held at Utica and a riot ensued. Delegates were driven from pillar to post and were insulted by a noisy, malignant mob. Conferences were held at the Court House, Dutch Reformed, First Presbyterian and Baptist Churches by those early friends of human freedom. Finally it was arranged to hold a general convention October 31, at the Court House. But before it convened a protest was gotten up by its opponents, and of the most disgraceful scenes ensued that ever darkened the fair pages of our history. The mind of the patriot is filled with disgust as we look back upon it from these enlightened days of human progress. The convention finally met at the Bleecker Street Presbyterian Church but was broken up and the participants compelled to adjourn to the village of Peterboro. It was well for them that the Sheriff and Under Sheriff were Whigs and in sympathy with their righteous cause. More than a score of the drunken riot makers were arrested and indicted at the December Sessions. The ranks of the old-line Democrats and slavery advocates contained some of the most distinguished men of Utica and some of its officials. They were orderly but their influence created the mob.

GEN. LYMAN CURTISS.

Lyman Curtiss succeeded Willard January 1, 1838. He was a business man and greatly interested in the affairs of the county, and especially the city of Utica. His term was conducted in a quiet and business like manner. The criminal calendar was loaded down with felonies and misdemeanors. These were principally from the city and incorporated villages. At the Oyer and Terminer, October 11, 1839, occurred the trial of Robert Miller for murder. He was a resident of Water street, in the city of Utica, and loved his little brown jug, not wisely but too well. Barney Leddy was one of his warmest friends, and he too was fond of his liquor. They both took too much one night and quarrelled over a trifling matter. Millar grabbed a club and slew poor Barney. He then stripped the unfortunate victim of his drunken rage of all his clothing and stamped them in the mud in his cellar. Then taking the body he sought to burn it and destroy all evidence of his crime. He was however caught in time and indicted, tried and convicted and sentenced to be hung on the second day of December, 1839. A respite was granted for a few days and then he was executed in the jail yard at Whitesboro. Many dangerous and corrupt manipulations now crept into the politics of Oneida county.

THE LOOMIS FARM.

The notorious Loomis gang had long been growing in influence and power. They were a strong political factor for candidates of their liking. They had their followers in every part of Oneida county. Their hiding places were among the mountainous hills of northern Madison county and the dark cedar swamp on the Unadilla creek. There were also dens in the swamps above Rome and along Oneida Lake. Some of the family yet reside in that locality. All manner of stories are told of the iron clad oath with which they bound those admitted to the secrets of the gang. As much must necessarily be said of their exploits and lawless deeds, it may be wise to give some idea of their great Sangerfield farm, consisting of several hundred acres. The author had the last legal bout with them about a year ago. They and their descendants are now litigating among themselves. The great farm is being cut up and divided under proceedings commenced by Dexter E. Pomeroy for his two children, who are heirs and legatees of a part of the estate. The only original leader left on the farm is Plumb, who was indicted lately for forcibly taking possession of lands set apart to his nephew and nieces. We received our papers, and as Plumb had threatened to dispose of any one setting foot on the soil of the old farm, we took an assistant and Surveyor with us so as to be sure and not trespass on any

lands not covered by our process. Hiring a conveyance at Waterville we proceeded to the farm. After passing through the village the Surveyor pointed to a high hill south of us and said it was on the Loomis farm, and the house on the north side was the residence of Plumb Loomis. In the distance it looked like a sugar loaf. It was raining some and at times this hill would be hid from view by the pouring clouds. It is about five miles distant from the village and our ride was over hills and down the valleys. As we neared the place the Surveyor pointed to the dark cedar swamp stretching from Sangerfield in Oneida county many miles into Madison county. In viewing it from the outside it would seem to be impossible for any one to find stolen horses or property secreted in its midst. It is a fearfully dark, dismal swamp. We helped to survey parts of it for the purpose of the partition. On reaching the farm the Surveyor, who was an old resident of the town, pointed out the spot where stood the old family residence for years, the place of meeting in secret conclave. Nothing now remains of the building but the blackened walls and closed ruins. In front is the tree where "Wash" was hanged until dead by the infuriated mob a score and a half years ago. Near by is the limb where Plumb was hung and left for dead at the same riot. The fences and bushes have been cut and splintered by curiosity seekers during the years gone by. The house stands at the junction of the road leading from Plumb's residence on the slope of the hill and the main road leading to Madison. We put out our team at the farm house beyond and proceeded to survey the farm and dispossess Plumb and his tenants. Commencing on the top of the hill with the clouds beneath us, we righted our compass and chained to the midst of the great swamp in the valley. Here we met Plumb and several men. He was in a rage and belched forth a war of angry words. When we advanced to make the arrest, in case of resistance they all retired. This was Plumb's first retreat and complete surrender. Afterwards he came armed with rifle and ax to retake part of another piece for which he stands indicted.

After he had retired we gave legal possession to Harry Morgan, the purchaser. The hill spoken of, overlooking the surrounding country, was a good place to watch the approach of hostile parties. It is said that when the Loomises were in their prime and the vote of Oneida county very close, that they controlled its candidates, some times in one party and sometimes in another. They were well educated and out of one of the best New England families Why they became criminals no one can tell. The only excuse given is that the excitement is fascinating. This is the excuse of almost every criminal. We shall speak of the events connected with this family as they occurred under the different Sheriffs of Oneida county. Other counties on the south had a similar experience. Their political distinction and approaching poverty is a warning to all men who seek by such means to get notoriety, power and riches, and by unlawful means obtain the obnoxious title of an infamous hero.

DAVID MOULTON.

Perhaps no man in Oneida county had a more extensive personal acquaintance than Col. David Moulton. He was Military Commander, Supervisor, Legislator and Sheriff. David's life experience was varied and eventful, both as farmer, politician and business manager. Few lawyers could equal him in the trial of a case, few possessed his genius and skill. He was sharp and sarcastic and full of wit and humor. As leader of the Democracy he seldom failed in a canvass. His motto was "anything to win" and "to the victor belongs the spoils." At times this sentiment seemed to drown his sense of public honor. He assumed the office and duties of Sheriff in the month of January, 1841. Socially he was a charming success, but as an executive a failure. He located the office at Rome and entered upon the discharge of his duties. For several years the celebrated McLeod case had occupied the attention of the American people, and for several years the United States and British Governments were in conflict as to the rights of the accused. Alexander McLeod was indicted in Niagara county for burning the Steamer Caroline and murdering one of her crew at Schlosser and then running the boat over Niagara Falls, December 30, 1837. He was a British subject and claimed the protection of the British flag. His government granted his request and engaged Joshua A. Spencer, of Utica, to defend him. Spencer was at the time United States District Attorney for Northern New York. A long controversy grew out of this as to the right of a commissioned officer of the government to defend a foreign subject where questions were involved that might call for a resort to arms. These discussions may be found

in the State papers of Governor William H. Seward, President John Tyler and the eminent Secretary of State, Daniel Webster. Also in the history of the trial. They are voluminous and extensive. At one time during the proceedings General Scott was ordered to take command of the troops in this State and repel the threatened invasion. The Chief Justice of the State and the Attorney General were directed to appear as Judge and prosecutor. But finally Mr. Spencer succeeded in getting a change of venue and trial in Oneida county. The prisoner was then removed from Lockport to the jail at Whitesboro. Sheriff Moulton now had the care and custody of the prisoner. In this case the State paid the expenses of the Sheriff and thirty extra deputies. Under the proclamation of the Governor a voluntary company of artillerymen, consisting of one hundred men, was organized in the county The militia was put under marching orders and the jail was constantly guarded. The author's father, Captain Thomas Bielby, was in command of one of these companies. Whitesboro was quite a military headquarters. Military officers of the United States Regular Army were also present. Spies from a Canadian band of patriots and squads of armed men were reported by the Sheriff to be prowling about the county, and some of them were encamped in the forests near Utica.

It was also reported to the British government that an armed band of men from the frontiers were marching to Utica to release and murder McLeod. This compelled the Secretary of War to see that the prisoner was properly guarded and protected. Finally the case came on for trial in the Academy at Utica before Hon. Philo Gridley, the County Judge and the Justices for the Sessions. Hon. J. L. Wood, District Attorney for Niagara county, and Hon. Timothy Jenkins, for Oneida county, represented the State. Gardner and Bradley were attorneys, and Hon. Joshua A. Spencer counsel for the prisoner. The name of the man murdered on the burned boat was Amos Durfee. The trial lasted several days; thirty-three witnesses were sworn for the people and fourteen for the defense. This was Mr. Spencer's greatest case and won for him a great reputation in England. He secured an acquittal of the prisoner. It was a very expensive proceeding for the State and National Governments, and at one time, when the British Government assumed the responsibility of the case, threatened a war with

England. This great trial and the other duties of the hour was a great temptation to Sheriff Moulton to make money. The affairs of the Sheriff's department became complicated and suspicious. Various complaints were made and finally charges preferred to the Governor. One charge was that he neglected his duty and revealed the finding of an indictment to a prisoner after a requisition had been issued. and for a monied consideration on a pretended settlement, and then allowed the prisoner to escape. For this Governor Seward, who issued the requisition, removed him from office. There was apparently much questionable practice between Moulton and the prosecuting officer. The Governor removed six sheriffs and other officers the same year. A full record of the proceedings may be found in the State papers of William H. Seward and the memoirs written by his daughter. Gov. Seward was a great man and model Governor. Moulton's light as Sheriff went out ingloriously, and as the Governor says for want of moral honesty. It is but just to say of this able and in many respects brilliant man that the electors were largely to blame. There was a looseness in party management and the corrupt use of money that led to these things and caused his official embarrassment The Loomis' and other gangs of corrupt men were courted for their numerical strength in votes. Such organizations should be discountenanced by all parties and denounced. Any candidate who will cater to the low, criminal elements to gain power will make an unsafe and dangerous official. The Sheriff's office never should fall into such hands. He can shield the bad and prevent their punishment or turn them loose to plunder the community. He should be a capable and honest man, with fixed principles and a determination to execute all processes of the courts without fear or favor, yet without extortion, fraud or oppression. We have learned of whole counties caused to be bonded by bad Sheriffs catering to lawless, riotous persons and permitting destruction of property. The value of property depends upon the protection given it by law, as well as invested labor or wealth. If the law is not respected and rigidly enforced, the products of toil and the savings of centuries may be swept away in a few hours. Aye, even insurance companies may be broken down and dissolved. Intelligence, honesty and integrity are the foundation of our government. Moulton was once independenly rich, but his fortune gradually disappeared, until came the great financial crash which swept his estate away and caused his ruin.

THEODORE S. FAXTON.

Away back in the early days of the nineteenth century there came to Utica a poor, penniless hard-working boy. His first employment seemed to have been upon the public streets. He was poor indeed in this world's goods, yet rich in integrity and sterling worth. And from the beginning he was honest and upright in all his dealings. Men trusted him because they believed in him; they employed him for his fidelity to their interests and firm convictions of eternal truth. On the removal of David Moulton, such a man was sought by Governor William H. Seward to fill the office of Sheriff of Oneida county, and such a man was Theodore S. Faxton. He was at once commissioned by the Governor and entered upon the discharge of his duties. He had been a permanent resident of the city and village since 1812. At that time he was a stage driver and held the reins until 1817, when he commenced to engage in other occupations. In 1825 he consented, however, to drive six dashing grays when attached to the carriage that bore General La Fayette to the grand reception given in his honor by our loyal citizens. The great and noble deeds of this noble man are still fresh in the memory of our people. He was ever on the watch to do good and advance the cause of science and Christian civilization He was one of the earnest men who developed the great invention known as the magnetic telegraph. There is hardly an industrial enterprise in Utica but what bears the impress of his genius and skill. Her woolen and cotton mills, her Faxton Schools and Faxton Homes, Masonry, Odd Fellowship, the Christian churches, and last sleeping place of the faithful dead, all reveal grand evidence of his love for his adopted home and Christian benevolence. He was in full political sympathy with the great War Secretary and gloried in the achievement of his party as it moved forward in the full front of human progress and human freedom. His appointment removed the office from Rome to Utica. As Sheriff, he was a grand success. His term was short, but it was brilliant and sparkled with Christian truth and love of justice. With him as Sheriff, people honored the office, and the law was respected and obeyed. And so it is in all things, when good men have power, the wicked tremble, and life and property, and all our sacred franchises, are secure and safe.

ISRAEL S. PARKER.

When Governor Bouck succeeded Seward and was duly installed in the Gubernatorial chair, he appointed Israel S. Parker of Rome, to take the place of Faxton as Sheriff of Oneida county. Faxton had not been removed and there was not the slightest cause for his removal except his politics. This renewed the great political battle between Rome and Utica, and it seems it has been raging ever since. The affairs of the office now became very complicated. Parker's commission was dated January 13, 1843. He duly qualified by filing his bonds and taking the oath of office. A notice of his appointment and qualification duly certified by the clerk, were duly served upon Faxton with a demand for the possession of the office. Then came a long and expensive litigation. The principal point involved was as to the right of the Governor to displace Faxton by appointing a successor without formal charges being preferred. The facts in the case and opinion of the learned Chief Justice, may be found in the 6th of Hill reports, at page 49. The court sustained the appointment. This removed the Sheriff's office back to Rome. No other matters of great historical significance occurred during Parker's term as Sheriff. A bitter political campaign followed between the rival county seats. This campaign resulted in the election of Palmer V. Kellogg, of Utica, for Sheriff of Oneida county for the ensuing term.

PALMER V. KELLOGG.

It would be hard to find in the city, county or State, a more successful business man than Palmer V. Kellogg. He was a man of fine presence and pleasant address. Few men succeeded better in the business world. His shrewd and ingenious scheming to foil and outwit a competitor is without parallel in mercantile enterprises. Hundreds living to day will remember his great clothing stores in Franklin Square and on the east side of Genesee street, below the bridge. His ambition was to succeed in life and make money, and he succeeded. He entered the political arena with the same motto and the same methods. In this he succeeded once and then failed. With his money he sought to organize the saloons and liquor elements in his favor, thinking they had power to carry him through.

Thousands of dollars were banked in this way and thousands of dollars were sunk with no return. Others delivered the goods that brought him votes. To enable his managers to carry out his designs he invented what is known as the "eel skin" or paster. Out of this has grown the tissue paper and other ingenious devices. He was elected Sheriff in 1843, and in the following January duly entered upon the discharge of his duties. A large share of the business during his uneventful term was done by deputies. Being ambitious to gain favor with the people he was liberal with his patronage and generous with his money. He wanted to go to Congress, but the lamented and honored Roscoe Conkling was now rapidly climbing the ladder of fame, and was the idol of the masses. In after years they were pitted against each other, Conkling on the regular Republican ticket and Kellogg on the combination. Conkling was elected and this blasted Kellogg's ambition for political favor. He returned to his business and prospered for a time in Utica and then removed to Chicago. Here he amassed a fortune and became one of its most esteemed business men. He lived to a good old age and died crowned with riches and honor.

LESTER BARKER.

In January, 1847, Lester Barker, the genial and happy drover, of Clinton, having been elected, duly qualified and assumed the responsibility of Sheriff. He was deservedly popular and well thought of by citizens, Bench and Bar. His election seems to have quieted, for a time, the jealousy between the halfshire County seats. He retained the office at Utica. His election turned the office over to the Democrats. By being careful and judicious in selecting his subordinates, and prompt in the transaction of business, he acquired the reputation of being a cautious and prudent official. His term in many respects was exciting and full of interest.

In addition to the Court of Sessions and Oyer and Terminer, the Recorder's Court of Utica had been established with criminal jurisdiction for the city of Utica. At a term of this court held in August, 1847, Mary Runkle was indicted for murdering her husband, John Runkle, while he was sleeping at their home on Corn Hill. Grand juries then sat in connection with the Recorder's Court for the indictment of felons. They also sat with the Sessions, but for some reason they are now discontinued in both. There should be at least one Grand Jury with the Sessions in September. The our terms of Oyer and Terminer are insufficient for the business of the county. From the May to the November term is too long for the confinement of poor prisoners unable to get bail. After indictment the Runkle case was at once sent to the Oyer and Terminer for trial. The trial resulted in a conviction. She was a desperate and unscrupulous woman. Suspicion and rumor had condemned her for several other murders in the county. The proof in this case established the facts that she seized her husband, while he was sleeping by her side in the middle of the night, and held him by the throat until dead. They were covered by utter darkness: there was no light in the room. Believing it safe she called her daughter a young girl, about thirteen years of age, to her assistance. There was her mistake, for this made the fatal proof that lead to her conviction. Her defense was that her husband died in a fit. Many stories have been told of her desperate deeds and attrocious murders prior to this. It is said that she killed and robbed two peddlers while they were asleep in her domicile at her home; also her two little innocent children by drowning them in a wash tub. She was finally executed by the Sheriff. Nov. 9, 1847, at the county jail, at Whitesboro.

No influence, rewards or threats could ever induce her to make a confession of her crimes

There were several other cases, but no convictions for murder in the first degree.

THE ROME COURT HOUSE BURNED.

The Court House at Rome was now destroyed by fire and another structure was built on the same site. In rebuilding the walls were constructed of brick, and the jail cells were of lime stone. The new jail and present structure has since been built by a Committee of the Board of Supervisors.

In the good old days, Sheriffs had charge of the erection of county buildings under the direction of the Courts. The Supervisors were then disinterested auditors of accounts, when duly verified and approved. The judges were careful in making their orders and prudent in creating expense. It was business not politics. Now we have large and expensive committees from the Board of Supervisors. It would seem to us that the Sheriff is the custodian and responsible man in the premises, and should be yet held responsible. When responsibility is so divided its usefulness is gone. The Sheriff is bonded for care, prudence and discretion. His oath is to the same effect and Grand Juries inspect his work under the direction of the Court. The Governor holds him strictly to an accounting, and the people have their civil remedy. Sheriff Barker was a good officer and prudent custodian of the people's property, and guarded all their interests with a zealous care He left the office with the entire confidence and esteem of the people.

JOHN R. JONES.

John R. Jones, of Whitestown, succeeded Barker, January 1, 1850. He was a successful business man and popular politician of his town, but he does not seem to have fully realized the great responsibility and complications of the Sheriff's office. He soon became entangled in some very costly and annoying litigation, which caused him great embarrassment and it is said financial ruin. He was, however, a kind man and good Sheriff, and made the best of the conflicting condition of things.

GREAT FIRES IN UTICA.

These were exciting times for the Sheriff's office For a long time the citizens of Utica had been alarmed by the many and increasing destructive fires. Building after building had been swept away until thousands of dollars had been wiped out of existence, and life itself endangered in many cases. Something must be done and the Sheriff was appealed to for assistance. For a time it seemed as if nothing could stay the spread of conflagration, waste and ruin. Guards were appointed to watch the city while detectives were engaged in ferreting out the crime and finding the evil doers. Finally suspicion pointed to a band of incendaries in the rival fire companies of the city. Some of them were the sons of wealthy men who lived in ease and luxury at home. Evidence rapidly accumulated against them until the chain was full and complete. Then came the indictment, arrest and tears. The rich and influential could not believe their boys guilty of such foul deeds. Chapters might be written on the crimes and the influence of the ,reckless on the public mind, the times

When, alas! Our guardian sleeps,
Vice claps her hands an virtue weeps

Indictments were found against James J. Orcott, Sarah Duffery, Henry Newell, Daniel Butterfield, Horace B. Conkling and others. Two of them were sent to states prison for life, but were afterwards pardoned by Governor Horatio Seymour. Others were sent for shorter terms and some fled for parts unknown. The indictment against Daniel Butterfield was dismissed by the Court on motion of his counsel, but poor Horace B. Conkling in the minds of many, less guilty but the most unfortunate of them all, had to suffer the fate of the condemned on the scaffold. Easily influenced, weak and subject to temptation, he yielded to his folly for their sport and paid the penalty with his life. Someone had to be crucified, he was chosen. He was legally put to death at the jail in Whitesboro, November 21, 1851. Sheriff Jones acted wisely in all these things.

OTHER CASES.

The next important case was that of John Perkins, of Sangerfield, for murder. He was convicted of manslaughter. Then came the case of William Harlon and Michael O. Sullivan, but in these, also, the District Attorney failed to maintain the charge of murder in the first degree. These were busy days for the courts, and lively times for the Sheriff and his staff. The tide of crime was checked for a time, and then broke out again in all its original fury. Sheriff Jones did his full duty and received the applause and congratulations of the people.

THE CAMPAIGN OF 1852.

The political campaign of 1852 was one of the most interesting of any in the history of the Empire State. Temperance reform in connection with the great abolition movement, had become the great, overshadowing issue of the day. Old inhabitants will recall with pleasure the Washingtonian movement that swept with such power through the land. Others will remember the Sons of Temperance and the Knights of Jericho. But the society of the most historical interest was the Good Templars, organized in Utica by Rev. Wesley Bailey, Leverett E. Coon, Hon Thomas L James and others. It has since become the most prosperous temperance society in the known world, and has spread into every continent and to the islands of the sea. Two years later the temperance candidate, Myron H. Clark, carried the State. His cause was championed by the rising young statesman, Roscoe Conkling, seconded by the Hon. Thomas L. James and other brilliant young men.

HUGH CROCKER.

In this great struggle Hugh Crocker, the Democratic candidate for Sheriff, was elected, and in January, 1853, assumed the duties of his office. Mr. Crocker was one of Utica's most active and shrewd business

men. He was a butcher by trade, and for a time kept the City Market. Genial and pleasant in manner and accommodating with all his patrons, he secured a very large and loyal circle of friends. Though kind in heart yet he was decided and prompt in action. He was just the man for Sheriff in the trying times of the hour. Being very careful and discreet in the selection of his deputies, he rallied around him a faithful and competent band of subordinates. No Sheriff was better fitted or equipped for the important work before him. To lead a fight against the lawless band that then threatened the fair name of Utica, required a man of sound judgment, a man of thought. Diplomacy, as well as executive ability was much needed.

One of the first and most valuable appointments he made was that of his brother and co worker, John G. Crocker, as Attorney and counselor for the Department. John G., at once set to work to master the laws and statutes and conflicting decisions pertaining to the duties of Sheriff. He did master them and did it well. The result was that he not only made the most complete briefs ever used in our courts, but produced the most reliable work on Sheriffs then in existence. His digest of decisions is yet used in almost every valuable work on Sheriffs, Coroners and Constables. Recent statutory enactments have changed the practice and made a new work necessary, but Crocker's work is valuable still.

THOSE FIRE BUGS AGAIN.

After having informed himself thoroughly on all the duties of the office, the new Sheriff at once proceeded to rid the city of the remaining fire bugs. Their reckless and destructive burning of buildings had produced a reign of terror. At the April Oyer and Terminer, John Miller, Seymour George, Patrick Larkin, William McCann, Montiville Smith and others were indicted. The sentences of those convicted varied from that of Miller for ten years and one month to five years for others Seymour George was acquitted. The Grand Jury indicted a large number of criminals at this term, among them Daniel L. Simmons for murder He was finally bailed by his counsel in the sum of $20,000. Hon. Roscoe Conkling and Hon. Ward Hunt were his counsel and surety. The bond was forfeited at the next term of court Then followed the indictment of Henry Schrader for murder, who was also defended by Conkling. Also John Bezold. Conkling was the bright and rising star among the lawyers of the county. The record sparkles with his brilliant achievements. Following these murder cases, came the brutal drunken affray at Boonville in which James McCann slew James O'Brien with a dagger. McCann was tried and convicted of murder in the first degree, and sentenced to be hanged December 15, 1854. He seems to have been reprieved by the Governor.

The Loomises had now grown bold and desperate again. Indictments were found against William W., George and Grove for grand larceny. The Sheriff did all that could be done to secure their apprehension and punishment, but their political power and money stayed the iron hand of law. Crocker's term proved trying and eventful, but was conducted with prudence and care. He was one of the best executive officers ever honored with the trust. The law was fearlessly enforced, and all the business managed with ability and success.

CALVIN HALL.

Calvin Hall, the brick manufacturer of Deerfield, succeeded Crocker in January, 1856. He followed in the footsteps of his predecessor and relied upon his business qualifications to carry him through. His first capital case was that of Catherine Jones, who was tried for murder and convicted of manslaughter and imprisoned at Sing Sing. Then, in quick succession, came that of Hugh Orr, the inhuman monster who beat his wife, Rachael Orr, while in a beastly state of intoxication, until she died. He was given seventeen years at Auburn. The cases of Charanda Youlan and Nicholas Acker for manslaughter, were then considered by the Courts. During Hall's term the indictments against the Loomis' for minor offenses cover pages of the record. Their depredations had so rapidly increased that the people were ready to rise in arms against them. Hall managed the office with much business skill and ability.

WILLIAM J. M'COWEN.

The Loomises had become so powerful, and increased in numbers and voting strength to such an extent that they bid defiance to all law and civil institutions. They were a band of lawless men proclaiming personal liberty and denouncing civil liberty. To bring them to justice and test the power of civil authority, the Republican convention nominated for its candidate the venerable and popular William J. McCown, of Sangerfield. He was elected by a handsome majority. He was in every respect a representative man of the county. Tall and graceful in form, noble in appearance, high minded in thought, commanding in presence, no better selection could have been made. His very presence would command respect and obedience. Socially he was one of the most pleasant men we ever met. The Loomises knew their fate was sealed unless they ceased hostilities. He cared nothing for their influence or political power; he was fighting for home and friends.

JAMES FILKINS.

To assist in carrying on the aggressive work against this lawless band he appointed the fearless and brave James Filkins as one of his general deputies. Filkins was a faithful officer and no process ever placed in his hands went unserved. He followed the Loomises through the cedar swamps, forests and dens. Many times resistance came and often with force of arms. In some of these combats he was dangerously wounded several times, and once pierced with a rifle ball. The author has often heard him relate his exploits with these desperate and unscrupulous men. The story of his experiences would fill several volumes. Sometimes the courts are slow to act and allowed such cases to go over the term on the slightest pretenses of counsel. So it was in the Loomis trials, until finally the outraged people became weary of slumbering justice and arose in their might to take the law in their own hands and to avenge their wrongs.

THE BATTLE.

Both parties had been preparing for the battle, but the Loomises were now on the defensive. Several were wounded on both sides But the people got the best of it and drove their long dreaded adversaries into their homes and hiding places. The gang now appeared before the Sheriff and claimed protection. Notices were served and processes of the courts placed in his hands—making the county liable for all damages in destruction of property. This did not stop the infuriated people; they continued the attack until the lawless desperadoes pleaded for mercy. The battle was a desperate one and the enraged people would not yield for a moment until they had accomplished their purpose.

THE MILITARY CALLED OUT.

Sheriff McCowen was now placed in a trying position. His neighbors and most intimate friends were the aggressors. It would be terrible to stay them by civil or military force. But he was Sheriff and the county must be protected if it called for the armies of a nation. No civil officers could handle such an overwhelming force. He was obliged to call out the military. The thought was terrible but it must be done. He issued his order and the forces assembled. But before they reached the field of action the rioters were dispersed. What a scene met the Sheriff's gaze as he and his staff approached the fatal spot! The buildings were aflame, the heavens were lurid with their light. Plumb had been hanged to a tree to make him confess his crimes and was nearly dead. No confession was wrung from him, however. George Washington Loomis, the leader of the gang, some time previous to this, had been killed with a slung shot in an altercation within the dales of the ill-fated homestead. Truly, in this case the mob was a monster.

FILKINS INDICTED.

James Filkins was indicted for this offence and for arson. He was put on trial, and after a long and expensive proceeding in the courts was acquitted. On the night of this fearful and unlawful assembly, he was acting with the Sheriff and endeavoring to prevent the destruction of life and property. But the Loomises took him for revenge and then sued the county for damages. They were, however, unsuccessful in the main but made some compromises. This is one of the cases that illustrates the dangers and sufferings of a faithful public servant. Filkins was ruined financially and suffered beyond all description from the fearful wounds he received. He is still living at his home near Waterville. It has been difficult to get an officer to serve in that locality ever since. Several have tried it but with fear and great caution.

MORE CASES.

There were several other cases of manslaughter in McCowen's term. We note the following: Seymour N. George, James Nolan, Jesse Sexton, George Lewis, Clark Lewis, William Rogers, Henry Budge and John Bachman. The indictment of the county board of Excise Commissioners for breach of official duty, caused much excitement. It was due to the same causes that have been repeating themselves in Town Boards and City Commissions ever since. The frauds and lack of public decency and personal honor in these bodies is without parallel in American institutions. The law and its intent is glaringly violated, and crimes under it winked at, and as the old sea captain said "when I signs them papers I turns my back."

GEORGE W. SMITH.

Another great and important event was the removal of the County Judge, George W. Smith, on the charge of bribery. Hon. Roscoe Conkling was the prime mover in these proceedings. A record of them may be found in his State papers and a brief sketch in the biography written by his nephew. They may also be found in the Congressional Record to some extent, as out of them grew the great fight between Conkling and Blaine. Perhaps we may be able to trace them even through many other campaigns and even to the defeat of the Presidential candidate in 1884. McCowen was a model Sheriff and is gratefully remembered by all who knew him. He was truly one of nature's noblemen

EIGHTEEN HUNDRED AND SIXTY.

The exciting political campaign of 1860 will long be remembered throughout the land. The Republican party was now well organized in Oneida county. A nomination was almost equivalent to an election, and 1860 was a Presidential year. The Republicans were united and in the race to win if possible. The Democrats were split asunder. For President the Republicans had Lincoln. The Democrats Douglass, Fillmore and Bell. The war cloud hung over us, the fate of the nation was trembling in the balance. There were Wide Awakes, there were Little Giants, there were Copperheads, there were Union men, there was Slavery, there was Freedom. Great, indeed, were the issues of those exciting times. The vote was all out. But on Sheriff all parties seemed to unite.

HUGH CROCKER AGAIN.

In this campaign Hugh Crocker was re-elected on a union ticket. He again duly qualified and entered upon the solemn duties of the office. John Bachman, who killed Conrad Lawrence, at Rome, October 6, 1861, was tried and convicted and imprisoned for life. The trial of William Rogers, who murdered his wife in the town of Vienna, immediately followed. He was convicted of murder in the second degree. A large number of indictments were found for assaults at elections. There were many Southern sympathizers in Oneida county. Some of them were rank and abusive. Following these came several great jail deliveries. Prisoners were aided to escape by their partners in crime, and some were released to enter the army. These were among the evils of the war. In the midst of it all came the indictments of Catharine Stannard, Clark Lewis,

Nathan Brigham and Thomas Kehoe.

THOMAS KEHOE

Kehoe was a desperate man when intoxicated. One day he had drank too much and on meeting · his neighbor, Michael Boilin, on the road from Westmoreland to Rome, they engaged in an altercation. They quarrelied and fought until Kehoe drew his knife and slew Boilin. In his anger he drove the dagger to his neighbor's heart; they had been friends, and when he became sober he regretted the deed and longed to make restitution. But the life he had taken he could not restore. He wept like a child, but the deed was done and his only consolation was what is done is done There was no calling it back. His friend was gone from his sight forever. All that was mortal was hid from his view in the darkness of the tomb. Boilin's family were indigent and left in poverty. Kehoe had no means but was finally released on bail by the order of Judge Bacon. He at once enlisted in the army, and it is said gave his bounty and his earnings to the family of the deceased.

OTHER CASES.

Norman Kimball and Napoleon Baromeough were also indicted for murder, and Henry Perry and Eliza Toleman for arson. About this time the famous ward politician, John Davy Hackett, was indicted for assault with intent to kill, but with his usual good fortune he soon satisfied the court he meant no harm. John was one of the police officers at the time and was one of the shrewdest of them all. He will be remembered as the political manager of the Fifth Ward of Utica. During this term Crocker added to his fame as a good executive officer, and was the last Sheriff to be re-elected.

HON. D B. DANFORTH.

January 1, 1864, Hon. D. B. Danforth, of Annsville, qualified and took possession of the Sheriff's office. He was a tanner by trade and at one time well provided with this world's goods, but in later years became addicted to the drink habit and died a victim of misfortune. In the hour of temptation he built castles in the air, and indulged in foolish speculations, one of which was a mammoth hotel in the oil regions. In politics he was an ardent Republican as the times then stood. At the first term of court when he officiated, Henry Murray was convicted of arson and sent to States Prison for eighteen years and three months for burning the house of Charles Latham in the city of Utica Patrick Kelley, John H. Yoult, William Jones, Theodore Webb, James Dillon and Henry Kent were indicted for other offences. Dillon was at once tried and convicted and sent to States Prison at Auburn. He was a bold, dangerous and desperate fellow, having set fire to the house of Undersheriff Glen Petrie at Rome. In 1866 Richard Jones was indicted for murder and successfully defended by the late D. C. Pomeroy, perhaps the most eloquent advocate of Oneida county's bar. Indictments were also found against Cury Coughlin and James Welch for murder, and John Comstock and Julius Martin and Martin A. Verer for arson. There were a few other indictments and convictions for lesser crimes, otherwise nothing seemed to occur out of the usual course of business in Danforth's term.

GEORGE F. WEAVER.

George F. Weaver, of Deerfield, became Sheriff of Oneida county, January 1, 1867. He was a descendant of the old Dutch family that helped colonize the town in which he lived. They were loyal in all the great struggles for American independance. He was loyal to preserve the union. By occupation they were farmers and brick makers. Their extensive yards are known throughout all Central New York From early manhood he had been identified with all the popular movements to benefit the county. His liberal hand was felt in every enterprise to benefit our charities our schools and our churches. His acquaintance was extensive and he was esteemed by all who knew him. In politics he was an ardent Republican and as such was honored with many positions of public trust. For years he was Supervisor of his town, Commissioner of Excise for the county and finally Sheriff.

His genial smile, his affable maners, his kindly disposition won for him the friendship of the masses both rich and poor. He was loyal and true to the best interests of all. In the stirring times of war he was for the Union and the freedom of the down-trodden and oppressed. He knew the cost of human liberty, he had learned it from his patriotic sires. It was the lesson of his childhood. The Weavers and the Bellingers were all patriots.

He entered upon the discharge of his duty as Sheriff to do right and oppose the wrong. The most important part of the oath to him, was not to commit evil, but to avoid deceipt, fraud and oppression. All men have made some mistakes and so did he, but they came through the overflowing kindness of his generous heart. He was one of the noblest public spirited men we ever met.

HIS FIRST COURT.

At his first term of court Hugh Moore was indicted for arson and James McQuade and Henry Carr for neglect of official duty. This apparently proved a political farce. There were also a large number of indictments for violating the excise laws. The complaints were made by the Law and Order League of the county. At this time a great temperance revival was in progress under the auspices of the Good Templars. They were then a powerful organization, and the individual members made themselves felt in the political world. M ny of the rising young men of to-day were brought into public life through their efforts. *The Temperance Patriot* published at Utica, was the official organ. In this movement the author first appeared before the people as an advocate. Hugh Moore was duly arrested and tried for arson and imprisoned. He burned Ezra Clark's buildings at Kirkland. A. Verter was tried and convicted He set fire to John Herbert's slaughter house in Deerfield. James Welch was tried for killing John Long at Utica. He was convicted of manslaughter and sent to Auburn. A powerful gang of burglars and robbers had long been operating at Utica, they were now broken up and several of them sent to view the status of Copper John. Dewitt and Jeremiah Tooley were jailed for arson and indicted.

WILLIAM HENRY CARSWELL.

Then followed the brutal and shocking assault and murder of Anbey Elizabeth Sanders at Annsville by William Henry Carswell. Atbey was but a child, young, innocent and virtuous. Carswell was a miserable, low, treacherous, craving liber tine The story of this awful crime has often been repeated in the public press, and exists in pamphlet form, a copy of which we have. In those days zealous publishers took advantage of public execu tion to make money by selling a printed record of the criminal and crime. It is poor reading and miserable trash, pollut ing everything with its foul presence and its touch. No mind can grasp it and be made better. The details are so shocking and repulsive to every sense of decency that I will not reproduce them here. It is sufficient to say he shamefully and cruelly violated her person, maimed and lacerated her body with a knife, crushed the bones in her side and back, beat out her brains with a stone and left her alone in the woods to die. He murdered her, and mutilated her body to escape conviction. But in his case justice was not slow

TRIAL AND EXECUTION.

He was at once indicted and tried. Fargo & Barnett, of Rome defended him. The record of his conviction may be found in the November Oyer and Terminer, 1868, and January 8, 1869, the execution oc curred at the Rome jail. The cold and heartless, barberous wretch.smarting under the sting of an awakened conscience, groaning with fear as he heard the sound of the workmen's hammer building the scaffold, shuddering with the thought of the pains and sufferings of the execution, trembling at the gates of death and the great punishment that awaited him in the eternity beyond, begged of the physicians in attendance to administer chloroform be fore the fatal drop should fall in the hours of his agony. The condition of the culprit's mind being such as to cause great trouble, the physicians yielded to his appeal and administered the drug. Then the victim of his own pasions, the vicious monster, the debased madman was no more. The drop fell, he was dead and his wicked mind and dangerous presence banished from the world forever.

CHARGES AGAINST THE SHERIFF.

Out of this execution grew many harsh and unkind criticisms against the Sheriff. Public sentiment divided on permitting the use of chloroform. Charges were pre sented to the Governor against the Sheriff, but on a careful examination of the facts he was fully and completely exonorated from all blame. It was intended as a kind and humane act on the part of the physi cian to stop the ravings of an angry and vicious mind.

HIS LAST TERM.

At his last term of court came the trial of Martha Hudson for arson in the first de gree. She set fire to the house of Leonard J. Kendall and burned it to ruins She was convicted in the second degree and committed to Sing Sing for life. There were a large number of trials for felonies and misdemeanors in all of which the Sheriff did his duty.

Sheriff George F. Weaver will long be remembered for his good qualities and un stinted benevolence. He was in every sense of the word a Christian gentleman. He lived to a ripe and good old age, and but a few weeks ago was laid away by loving hands in his final sleep, amid the cheerful shades and fragrant flowers of Forest Hill Cemetery. He sleeps well. For

The ashes of the just.
Smell sweet and blossom in the dust.

LEWIS GAYLORD.

At the general election of 1870 Lewis Gaylord, of Rome, was duly elected Sheriff of the county, January 1, 1871, he duly qualified and entered upon the discharge of his duty. He is a business man of the ancient city and keeps a meat market. Political y he is a Republican, and at the time of his election was a leader in the party. He had served as Deputy Sheriff and was well qualified for the duties of the office. The main office was now located at Rome again and after the lapse of many years.

HUGH MALLON.

The first great trial in his term was that of Hugh Mallon for the murder of George B Porter in a saloon and gambling hell at Utica. In the first great trial of this case Daniel Ball, the District Attorney was assisted by Marshal B. Champlain the Attorney General of the State. The prisoner was represented by Pomeroy & Southworth of Rome. It is one of the celebrated cases on record. The trial took place at Rome and lasted several days. The arguments of the learned counsel and eloquent advocates were superbly grand. Daniel C. Pomeroy sumed up for the prisoner and the Attorney General for the people. Pomeroy's effort was one of the best of his life. His peroration on the value of human liberty, the life of a peer, the sacredness of the home, and the widows and orphans made sad by the verdict of a jury, was of the highest standard of forensic eloquence.

There was a beautiful tender, pathos in Pomeroy's voice that never failed to touch a juror's heart. He was a man of kindly disposition and tender sympathies. Opposing counsel wept, the widow sobbed aloud and the jury were in tears. Even the learned judge could not control the emotions of his heart's sympathies. But there was one tearless cheek, there was one undimmed eye, it was that of Marshal B. Champlain. The learned a lvocate turned to him and made an appeal for mercy, but there was no expression of feeling on his part. He had studied the case and listened to the evidence as detailed by the witnesses and was firm in his conviction of guilt. Nothing could move or sway him from what he believed to be the path of duty. When the counsel for the defense closed there was a ripple of applause. The Sheriff rapped to order. Champlain was a large man, of fine presence, and almost perfect in form. His hair had been dark and curly, but was now sprinkled with gray and fast whitening locks. When he

arose there was a painful and almost breathless si ence. He stood for a moment in the presence of the jury, and then commenced by saying he appreciated their sympathies for the prisoner and his family. Then pointing with his finger to the southern hills he remarked that in a rural home there sat a widowed mother waiting and weeping, but not for the return of their verdict, for that would not restore her boy, it would not remove the sorrow from her humble domicile or sadness from her aching heart. For her hope, her fond ambition, her staff in life was gone He had been stricken down by a reckless assassin, amid a lawless gang in the darkness of the night. To meet her boy she must look to the realms above. He then analyzed the evidence and brushed away the legal arguments of the defense like so many cob webs on the wall. The jury retired at the close of his powerful argument and returned with a verdict of murder in the first degree.

THE CASE.

The people of Utica and Oneida county will recall the details of this infamous crime, and the low gambling hell where it was perpetrated. Some of the participants are yet living. Mallon was sentenced to be hung, but the case was stayed on appeal, and a new trial granted. On the second trial the prisoner was convicted of manslaughter, and imprisoned at Auburn for a term of five and a half years. The murder was a brutal one and should be a warning to all young men to avoid such places of unlawful pleasure and amusement. There is always danger of a quarel where men are drinking and gambling for money. Porter was killed in one of these affrays by being hit with an instrument of death. His widowed mother was then left alone in the world, without his aid and support. The uncertainty as to who dealt the deadly blow saved Mallon's neck, but left a life of misery. His mental suffering was almost too great to bear, and darkness seemed to shaddow his pathway. To him the world lost its pleasures and its charms. He bore his affliction until death removed him hence.

CALLAHAN AND CAHOON.

The next capital case in the term of Sheriff Gaylord was that of Mary Callahan for killing her infant child at Utica. She was convicted and sent to Sing Sing. Then came the case of Daniel Cahoon for taking the life of his own wife at Bridgewater. He shot her in the side, shoulder and breast in a fit of drunken madness. Being deaf and dumb, and pleading pity ously for mercy in writing, and there being other extenuating circumstances.' he was allowed to plead in a lower degree, and sent to Auburn, to repent of his unnatural crime.

M'GEE AND EDIC.

Following came the case of Hugh McGee for killing Thomas Rowland with a stone, at the Chamberlain Zouaves' picnic at French's grove, New Hartford. This case will be remembered by many. Hon. Francis Kernan was counsel for the defendant. On the first trial the jury dis agreed, and on the second he was convicted of manslaughter, and imprisoned accordingly.

Eliza Ann Edic was tried, for beating her husband, Christian Edic, with a club until he died. The crime was committed at Sangerfield. She pleaded guilty to manslaughter and went to Sing Sing. All female prisoners from Oneida county were sent to this prison.

JOSEPHINE M'CARTHY.

We now come to the celebrated trial of Josphine McCarthy for shooting and killing George Hall, while quietly riding on a Genesee street car at Utica. Out of this case grew some of the blackest scandals that ever cast a shadow on American jurisprudence. The fair fame of Oneida county was dishonored There were several indictments for libel, the principal one being against Wilber Payne, for libeling the court and Judge Charles H. Doolittle by a prevaricated statement of its proceedings. Josphine undoubtedly did not intend to kill Hall, but how the mistake occurred has been a mystery. It is said by one of the passengers on the car that when she entered she was frenzied and desperate. One of the passengers saw the glittering revolver as she drew it from her muff, and by raising his arm struck her hand, and thus what might have been a deliberate murder became an accident, for she evidently intended to kill some one. The case was a very complicated one, and difficult to try. Eminent counsel was engaged by both sides. D. C. Stoddard, District Attorney, and Hon. Charles Sedgwick, appeared for the people and Lewis H. Babcock, Daniel C. Pomeroy and Hon. Charles Mitchell for the defense The result was an acquittal by the jury over which there was much speculation. Judge Doolittle was surprised at the verdict, and thought the jury had been packed to defeat the ends of justice.

HOW JURIES ARE PACKED.

The author has heard of such things being done in several cases, They were liquor cases. In one case the defendant had a young friend in the County Clerk's office, the clerk being the custodian of the box containing the names of jurors. The Grand Jurors are named by the Supervisors, the Trial Jurors by the Supervisor and Assessors of each town and ward. These boxes were taken down and a list of names selected and placed in the center of the box, and when the Clerk took the box to draw with the Sheriff and County Judge acting as inspectors, sufficient of the selected names were drawn to complete a pannel. Another way was this: The counsel agreed to go on with the regular pannel and then exhaust it, and called for talesmen. A list of names were placed in the hands of the officer, favorable to the defendant. This practice in justice's court is frequently indulged in, and in Recorder's Courts and Special Sessions. I mention these facts simply to illustrate how such things might be done. The learned Judge had an opinion of his own.

OTHER CASES.

Jacob Bernhardle was now tied for killing a boy in a masquerade at Rome. Charles and Joseph Harris were indicted for arson, and a large number for violating the excise laws. These were brought by the Law and Order League at Rome. Charles Suples was then indicted for killing Peter Conner at Rome. He was convicted of manslaughter. Thomas Buchanan, Cashier of the Peoples' Safe Deposit and Savings Institute of Utica, N. Y., was indicted for grand larceny and embezzlement. He was tried and acquitted.

WILLIAM J. PERKINS.

Oneida county has produced few young men who could equal the criminal record of William J. Perkins. Born in the town of Floyd, in 1848, and schooled in the streets of Oriskany and Utica, until the breaking out of the war, he picked up all the vices of the neglected street urchin. By trade he was a machinist and lather. When the war broke out he enlisted in the army and served faithfully to its close. He was a brave and kind-hearted soldier. If the record of his good deeds could stand alone, they would shine as a monument of glory. But he was unfortunate and yielded to temptation and fell. In a thoughtless moment he drank too much and his good deeds were lost to the world and obscured by darkness and shadow. He was first imprisoned in Utica jail for

intoxication. He was afterwards transferred to Rome, and while there made a
saw of an old knife, cut the bars and escaped with his brother to Port Leyden.
Cold weather came on and they were
obliged to seek for food to keep from
starving. While doing this they were
identifed and captured. They were then
brought back to Rome, bound hand and
foot with shackles and bracelets. He now
felt his disgrace keenly, and shuddered at
the approach of his friends. Now he
must answer an indictment for jail breaking and escape. The trial came on at
Rome and the jury disagreed. He was
then transferred to Utica and convicted.
Sentence was pronounced—ten months in
the Albany Penitentiary. Before it could
be carried into effect, he broke out of Utica
jail. This time by a saw conveyed to
him in a mince pie by a friend who never
forsook her boy—his mother. He escaped
to Boston, and was arrested and again cut
his way out before the requisition could
reach him from the Governor. He now
took refuge under the American flag,
enlisted in the United States marines and
went to sea. After serving five years he
came back to Utica. He was now arrested
in a saloon and sent to Albany to serve his
sentence. This was discouraging and
made him more reckless than ever He
was finally captured, indicted and convicted of burglary, and sent to the State's
prison at Auburn. There is no doubt
but that he was the most skillful burglar in Utica or Oneida county And had
the same genius and skill been applied
to some legitimate calling would have
made him what he appeared to be, not
what he really was. He came into the
world as free from vice as the rest of mankind. He possessed a noble heart and
every faculty of the noble man. Society
is greatly to blame for his downfall and
ruin. He learned the motto of the world,
but, alas! to late. It was: "Hit him hard,
he has no friends." He struck back, but
he lost, and lost all he had. This rounded
out the busy and successful term of Lewis
Gaylord.

GEORGE BENEDICT.

The canvass of 1873 was a stormy one.
The Republican party was yet in the as-
cendency but was divided into factions.
Some were Liberals, some Greenbackers
and many Prohibitionists. In order to
elect their candidate he must be able to
hold these factions together. To add fuel
to the flame, Conkling and Ellis H. Roberts,
the recognized leaders, had disagreed. And

the veteran solders made their demand for
recognition. They must have a man on
the ticket. The County Clerk's office was
already in the hands of the Democrats
through this element by the election of
Major James Bronson, in the previous
campaign. A Sheriff and Clerk must be
elected if possible. The Clerk's office was
worth $20,000 for a term of three years,
and the Sheriff's over $15,000 for the same
time. Candidates were numerous and
the contests were bitter and unpleasant.
When the convention met at Rome in the
fall, a great political storm ensued. The
clashing hosts first met at the Court House
and then adjourned to Sink's Opera
House to accommodate the masses. After
wrangling and voting for hours George
Benedict, of Verona, was nominated.
Benedict was a well to-do farmer and especially well thought of by that element.
He was also a Christian gentleman and
took a great interest in the welfare of the
church. In short, he was an exemplary
citizen. In the factional differences he
was a Conkling man. He had represented
his town in the Board of Supervisors several terms and was well acquainted with
their workings. His acquaintance was
large and extended throughout the county.
The nomination was ratified at the polls
and Benedict was elected. But the factional fight continued, and the differences
could not be healed. January 1, 1874, he
duly qualified and entered upon the discharge of his duty. His term, from the
beginning, was full of trouble, anxiety
and perplexity. New and varied complications were arising all the time. He
was, however, fearless and determined to
make the best of the situation. But, like
a great many other Sheriffs he was unfortunate in the appointment of his subordinates. He removed to Utica with his family and retained the office here. In fact,
he tried to harmonize the factions, and in
that way disloyal men were placed upon
his staff. This was more noticeable in
Rome than elsewhere, especially at the
jail. They were oposed to him in sentiment, principle and the discharge of official duty. Such is the curse of politics
as now managed and the folly of candidates. All subordinates should be in full
political harmony with their principals.
Candidates should be competent and
honest and share the responsibilities of
their chief. There may be exceptions but
they are few and growing smaller George
Benedict and James Tanner are competent
to speak on this subject. A man had better be without an office than to allow his

appointments to be dictated by spoils-men who deal in the mercantile vote. Public positions should not be dealt in as merchandise. The sacred franchises of the people should not be abused either by rewards or bribes. It is wrong and the people should stamp it out and resent it at the polls. A party had better go to the wall rather than the sacred institutions of our government. Benedict tried to stay the tide when it was too late. We have said this much to pave the way for what follows.

CRIMINAL CASES.

The first capital case that called for the attention of Sheriff Benedict was that of Perrine Matteson, who killed his brother at Paris Hill in a fit of jealous anger. It was on a Sabbath morning when all things else seemed to be in harmony and keeping with the sacredness of the day. They had quarreled and Perine took his gun and hid in the barn until his brother approached him and then shot and killed him. He was finally declared insane and committed to the State Asylum where he now remains. Conrad Baker was indicted for burning buildings near Rome, and Samuel Haaeur was indicted for burning, as we are informed, what is called the Gardner Block at Utica, and Henry Trembly for arson at Whitestown. James Fetherston Petit was indicted for murder. He killed Catherine Fetherston Petit at Utica in a drunken row. It is said that he pounded the poor woman to a jelly. He was allowed to plead manslaughter and was imprisoned accordingly. Edward Mullen was indicted for killing James O'Neil with a whip stalk in the alley near Lowery's Knitting Mills on Bleecker street, in Utica. He was tried and convicted of manslaughter and sent to Auburn for four years. David White and Joseph Hayden were indicted for murder in the first degree. David K. Pierce and George Woodruff were convicted of arson in the first degree and imprisoned for life. They burned the dwelling of Charles L. Gibbs, at Sangerfield. In these days crime seemed to be rapidly on the increase, especially in Utica.

THE GERMOND BURGLARY.

For a long time the city of Utica had been infested with an organized gang of desperate burglars. Murder, arson, maiming, and crimes of every description were committed. The county authorities and Police and Fire Commissioners of Utica had taxed their ingenuity to the fullest extent to search out the perpetrators of these dreadful crimes. Spies were put to watch, and foreign detectives were employed by prominent citizens. It soon became evident that some of the city guardians were not entirely loyal to their official duty. Suspicion soon found its subject and then the traitor was sought to reveal the workings of the mysterious band. Some one was to be made a victim of a burglary. It is said the man selected to be the victim of this cruel scheme was Peter Germond and his inoffensive family. He lived south of the southeast corner of the city in New Hartford. The night of the burglary was agreed upon as arranged by the spy or pretended burglar and citizen. A band of staunch and loyal men were to be present and capture them in the act. But it so happened that the Vernon bank was to be robbed on the night previous. This was foiled by a fire that took place in Vernon near the bank the night before. For fear that the fire might break out again a watch was kept on all night. The burglars had their man on the ground who reported these facts. So they changed their plans and went to Germond's a night sooner than was intended. Germond was unprotected and defenceless. He had no knowledge of the cruel scheme being worked upon him. Like many other farmers he took little precaution in making the approaches to his residence safe. He retired with his family in the full confidence that all was well.

The headquarters of this infamous band was at a more infamous den near the banks of the Mohawk river. Here they met and divided their blood money and ill-gotten gain. Here they reveled in the lap of luxury. From here they proceeded to the banks of the Mohawk river opposite Third street and masked themselves for their hellish work. Then up Third street they went to Pleasant and from Pleasant to the unpleasant scene of action. Access to the house was easy, as a member of the family was yet in one of the outer buildings and the door was open. They proceeded to the room of Germond and ironed him with bracelets. His wife and children were confined in another room with a masked and armed robber on guard. They soon plundered the house and retired. Germond followed them to the city to be released from his iron bands. The alarm was given and an order to arrest any and all suspicious persons published. Rioting on their stolen plunder and congratulating themselves on their easy escape, the vile band scattered in all directions to avoid detection. Some of them went to their homes and some to the foul dens of ill-fame for unlawful pleasure. But one was too anxious to escape and hastened to the depot to take the early train. He believed himself unsafe.

WILLIAM J. CONROY.

He is soon arrested and proves himself to be William J. Conroy, captain of the Highland gang on the Hudson. Perhaps a more cruel and desperate man never lived. He was unscrupulous and heartless. He was put into the custody of the Sheriff and finally induced to tell the whole story of his shame. Interested citizens visited him at the jail and promised him his liberty and a reward if he would divulge the whole secret of his crime. It is done, and Conroy, a few days ago but a despised robber, is made the hero of the hour. He makes a clean breast of it and prides himself in his shame. The Grand Jury sits, he goes before it and the desperate gang headed by Thomas Scott, "Buckey" Malone, George Ellis and others are indicted, tried and convicted and given sentences aggregating nearly a hundred years. Conroy is now released on bail. The bail is forfeited, and one of the greatest farces ever known in the criminal jurisprudence of the criminal world is enacted.

WARRANTS FOR CONROY.

The parties promising Conroy his liberty and reward little thought of the dreadful character of the man. He was associated with a gang that had ransacked and robbed in almost every city and village east of Albany. Warrants were in the hands of the Sheriff demanding his presence in other counties. The Sheriff was responsible for their execution and his custody. Jailors and all deputies were notified of this fact and so was Conroy. Notwithstanding this an attempt was made to get him out of the custody of the Sheriff to use as a witness in the Hood burglary at Albany.

HIS ESCAPE.

The jailor at Rome was induced to bring him to Utica, and while the train was waiting at the depot, a lunch was provided for all. While the jailor was drinking his tea and eating his oysters, the train commenced to move, and Conroy and his would be custodian escaped to the train. The jailor ran and jumped on and jumped off. He repaired to the Sheriff's office for instructions and was instructed to go home.

The Sheriff, armed with his warrants, at once organized a posse to pursue the fleeing refugees. It consisted of the Sheriff George W. Benedict, Alexander Hutchinson and the author. The author was in Clinton all day, and returned just in time to be sent for. The main deputy being engaged, the writer was requested to accompany the party. The train which Conroy had taken only went as far as Little Falls. So the posse boarded the express and reached Little Falls shortly after the accommodation. The posse was to divide, two going on each side of the train from front to rear. We had hardly alighted from the car when a yell came from the shaded darkness on the river side like the howl of a Commanche chief. It was an indication that George W. Benedict had discovered Conroy.

THE BATTLE.

Proceeding to the spot from whence it came, behind a great caboose, a deadly fight was going on between young Benedict and three other men. At the time we did not know who they were, but were afterwards informed that one was Conroy, the others Detective Cower and Hon. Miles C. Comstock. Young Benedict took hold of Conroy with one hand and Comstock with the other. In a few moments revolvers were flashing in the lamplight. As the author approached with his handcuffs the combatants retreated to the train. Here another battle ensued, and it was a desperate one. There was a war of angry words and clash of weapons. Each party called upon the assembled crowd for assistance. The Sheriff and his posse were getting the worst of it. Blood flowed freely. A revolver was pointed at the author, and in an instant he wrenched it from the hand of his assailant. There were a few blows and a flash and Conroy lay bleeding in the arms of young Benedict. The affray was then soon ended and the assailants rushed from the car for their own dear life. We had met the enemy and they were ours.

CARING FOR THE WOUNDED.

The wounded prisoner was then taken to the hotel and a surgeon summoned. It proved to be an old chum of the author's. He probed for the bullet but could not find it. It had entered the cheek below the left eye and passed into the mouth. The wound was painful but not dangerous. After caring for the prisoner all took the morning train for home. Conroy was afterwards surrendered on a writ of habeas corpus and taken to Albany to testify in the cases there. He was afterwards bailed on the indictments against him and set free for a time. But he could not shake off his old habits—he was a natural criminal. He soon committed several great crimes in quick succession. He is said to have shot and badly wounded one of his female friends in a jealous passion, also to have shot and wounded an officer trying to arrest him, and finally he blew the front of a house to pieces at Hudson and was sent to Clinton Prison to die, that is for life, and he did die there.

HE SWORE HE WOULD KILL THE WRITER.

Conroy had sworn that he would kill the writer at sight for revenge. For this purpose he came to Utica and lay around for weeks and shadowed the object of his search wherever he went. One morning in June it became necessary to take the three o'clock train for the East. The author started down Genesee street to the depot. On approaching Bagg's Square who should he meet but Conroy. He was coming from a well known resort in Deerfield. Revolvers were drawn and a duel was apparent. Each party advanced within about ten paces. The author stopped and took deliberate aim and Conroy dropped and ran into Bagg's Hotel. He was a cruel and heartless sneak and blood thirsty villian. He thought the chances were against him and vanished from our sight. Thus ended the story of the great Germond burglary.

CHARGES AGAINST THE SHERIFF.

Among the prisoners in Rome Jail was Richard Dillon. He was indicted for setting fire to the buildings on Col. Enoch B. Armstrong's farm. Armstrong was eager and anxious for his conviction. Dillon was sickly and suffering from a fatal and offensive disease. Physicians advised that he be allowed to go out in the jail yard for his health as a matter of humanity to the prisoner and justice to his associates. The jailor at Rome permitted him to do so. One day Dillon made his escape. Armstrong was indignant and was determined to prefer charges against the Sheriff.

THE BOARD OF SUPERVISORS.

When the Board of Supervisors was about to convene, the Sheriff having to leave the county on important business, wrote letters to those whom he thought to be his friends with reference to the organization of the Board. Armstrong learning this, made it an additional charge, claiming t was done to pack the committee in his favor; that the Sheriff was an old Supervisor and knew who were liberal men. When the Board met a majority of the members named were placed on the committee. They were supposed to be honorable men who understood their duty.

THE COMMITTEE.

The committee met and organized. The Board was Democratic, as was a majority of the Committee. Chairman Silas T. Ives was an ambitious man and Assemblyman-elect. He was a friend of Armstrong and was playing hot and cold, but in fact was a deadly enemy of the Sheriff. Armstrong was a leading Democrat and had a great influence with the Board. Ives kept him posted on all seeming irregularities of the Sheriff's accounts. As each one was named Armstrong would note it and put it on his brief for charges. Finally the charges were perfected and preferred, Albert N. Borst, Supervisor from Bridgewater, and ex-Clerk, joining with Armstrong as complainant. The charges were briefly as follows:

SPECIFICATIONS AND TRIAL.

The escape of Dillon, attempting to pack a committee of the Supervisors in his favor, putting too many officers on the courts, exorbitant charges against the county and general misconduct. They conveyed to Governor Samuel J. Tilden, with a request that he appoint a commission to hear and take the evidence, and that the Attorney General or a Deputy be instructed to take charge of the case. The County Judge and District Attorney were both Republicans and friendly to the Sheriff. In compliance with the request, Hon. Arthur M. Beardsley was appointed Commissioner and D. M. K. Johnson, of Rome, Deputy Attorney General. A long and tedious trial ensued as the Sheriff answered the charges through Hon. J. Thomas Spriggs and the Kernans. A large volume of evidence was taken by the reporter for the *Utica Morning Herald* (William Schachtel, now of the *Press*) for Johnson & Prescott, which lies before me. This was submitted to the Governor. The Governor found substantially as follows: The escape of Dillon occurred through no fault of the Sheriff, but through the fault of a deputy, and, as the deputy was promptly removed by the Sheriff he had purged himself of any criminal or official negligence. The deputy should be punished.

Attempting to pack the Board of Supervisors and organize them in his favor. That indiscreet letters were written by his clerk, but the fact unsustained.

Putting too many officers on the courts. Not sustained, being more particularly the fault of the courts, as they had their right and it was their duty to have the roll called at the opening of the court and dismiss all unnecessary attendants. It made a great expense to the county, but as extraordinary trials were in progress like the Germond burglary, it must be assumed that the Court thought them necessary.

Exorbitant charges. Some of the charges were irregular but the Supervisors were there to audit and correct. The Sheriff had the right to place his own value on all services not provided for by statute, and the Supervisors were the arbitors of the true value, and as they had exercised that duty the responsibility was with them.

General misconduct. Not sustained.

Governor Tilden laid aside the case with his conclusions and his successor, Governor Robinson, dismissed them. The proceeding cost the county about $10.000. Three thousand was refunded to the Sheriff for disbursements. A full account of this case may be found in the printed volume of the trial and in the State papers of Governors Tilden and Robinson. The trial was very exciting and at times witnesses and even opposing counsel indulged in a war of words, and in the excitement one of the counsel for the defense assaulted one of the counsel for the prosecution.

MEN ENGAGED IN THE GREAT TRIAL.

When this great case was on trial, the author was managing clerk in the office of Johnson & Prescott at Rome. As such he aided in the preparation of the case and became familiar with the laws governing the duties of Sheriff. He had been, up to this time, carrying two and distinct courses of study—law and theology. Law with Johnson & Prescott, and theology with Professors of Hamilton and Auburn. He had worked his way through all the preparatory schools and invested what money he had saved in the old homestead farm of his ancestors. A great fire now occurred and laid in ashes nearly all the buildings on the estate, and swept away his earnings, unless the lands could be redeemed. All of his near relations but his mother and a younger brother had gone to their final rest. The affairs of the estate were complicated and the property left badly encumbered. Dark, indeed, seemed the future. But the homestead must be redeemed for mother Theology had to be dropped and law resumed, alone. It was a necessity, but from the depth of a grateful heart, to a kind and

beneficent Providence, may it be said and affirmed, we hope to so live as to cast what little influence we may have in the balance, where it will weigh and be counted in the cause of our Divine Master. We believe in His teachings and confide in His promises. For in the innermost soul there is a something which teaches us that they are true. It may be what Ingersoll calls the touching of the "Something deemed divine." Certainly it is an experience, a realization. While contemplating these things and the duty of the hour, Sheriff Benedict found us and sought our services. We were now admitted to the bar and accepted his proposition as deputy, clerk and counsel. Here we have remained ever since, under all the administrations and have succeeded. Succeeded in almost all we have undertaken; succeeded in redeeming the homestead; succeeded in erecting a shaft to the memory of the grateful dead and kind remembrance of our kindred; succeeded in building a home for ourselves; succeeded in everything but politics, and in that we have partially failed, and for this reason, to the unfortunate ones addicted to the vice of intemperance, we have acted the part of the "Good Samaritan." That is, we belong to a Temperance Society.

From this point we write not alone from the records, but from memory and personal experience. And when we say that, we can say, of George Benedict, that he was a well meaning and deserving Sheriff. He made some mistakes, and so have all the rest. These cost him much trouble and expensive litigation. The appointment of constables or attendants for the court is a political nuisance and has caused every administration as well as his much trouble and complaining. Many ward politicians, Supervisors and wire pullers often impose upon Sheriffs to secure their appointment. In January, 1889, the Judges of the Supreme Court fully appreciating this, met in convention under the law, and fixed the number, thus, relieving the Sheriff from most of the responsibility. By their action in such courts, the discretionary power of the Sheriff is largely taken away. The appointments are now made by order of the court, or only as fixed by the judges, and the rule is rigidly enforced. So the Courts assume the responsibility. Had this action been taken in Benedict's time much evidence would have been ruled out of the great trial. Many of the malignants could not have vented their feelings for revenge. Political soreheads are the most spiteful and unscrupulous of mankind. It is well for Sheriffs, taxpayers and all concerned, that the Courts have removed these appointments, at least, partially from politics.

D. MINOR K. JOHNSON.

It is a grateful and pleasant duty to pause right here, in the midst of these sketches, and pay a tribute of respect to one of our dearest and most revered friends, D. Minor K. Johnson, Deputy Attorney General in the Benedict trial. A man more devoted to his chosen profession never lived. He was ever true to his clients, and honest and scrupulous to a fault. Every case that came into his hands he he made his own. His books were his constant companion, and his selections were the very best and most reliable standard works. Socially he was genial and pleasant; he delighted in the student who was ambitious and faithful in his studies. Few graduated from his office who are not steadily climbing the ladder of fame. In the laws of negligence and co operative rights, he was master. He was careful, painstaking and clear upon every legal proposition. For years before his death, he was counsel and attorney for the N. Y. C. & H. R. RR. Company. He and Depew Sedgwick and Mitchell, all distinguished men, were school chums, and became advocates, orators and successful lawyers. Many of his cases, from the Circuit to the Court of Appeals, stand as monuments to his learning, genius and care. They will remain as guides to the profession for centuries to come, as precedents for generations yet to follow. He loved, he honored and adorned his profession. In his family he was a kind and indulgent husband and parent. He loved his family far better than himself. His standard of excellence was the most enobling, for it was the Christian standard. He lived and thought for the benefit of the world and his profession, and the world and profession was made better that he lived and thought. We have mentioned these facts because he was the prosecuting attorney in the Benedict case, and because he was our own tutor in the early days of our study. We entered his office a poor, wounded cripple, with little money and few friends. In our physical condition, we were unable to perform many of the duties of the office as it should be done, and he kindly aided and corrected, as fatherly as he would a child. He was a noble man, and will ever have in our mind and heart, a grateful and affectionate remembrance.

No wonder Governor Tilden and the States Attorney designated him for the responsibilities of the great Sheriff trail of Oneida County. He was eminently fitted

and did honor to the trust

CYRUS D. PRESCOTT.

Cyrus D. Prescott was the law partner of D M. K. Johnson, and now conducts the large railroad practice left to him as a legacy by the firm on the death of Mr. Johnson. He is a careful, painstaking attorney and has held many important positions of public trust, among them Commissioner, Alderman, Assemblyman and Congressman. Such were the counsel arrayed against Benedict.

THE DEFENSE

For the defense were associated the Kernans including Francis and William Kernan, E. D. Mathews and J. Thomas Spriggs, a grand array of legal talent. Few lawyers in Oneida County ever excelled in tact and skill, the genius of J. Thomas Spriggs. He was a most successful, pleasing and eloquent advocate. The untruthful witness seldom escaped his notice and detection and sarcastic rebuke. His life-work is yet familiar to us all. In politics he was Democrat and held various positions of trust among them Committeeman, County Treasurer, Mayor and Counsel for Utica and Member of Congress. Francis Kernan has long been eminent in his profession, and as a great lawyer enjoys the distinction of a national reputation. He has held many offices among them Congressman and United States Senator. His brother, William, and all his sons, share in the fame and distinction of the affair. Arthur M. Beardsley, the Commissioner is a son of the great Jurist, Samuel A. Beardsley, Justice of the Supreme Court, and was appointed for his eminent fitness. This great trial revolutionized the Sheriff's office, and its influence has been felt throughout the State. Almost every year the author has gone to the legislature for the correction of abuses. Some of his briefs have aided in bringing about changes in the counties and cities. More especially for imprisonment under civil process. In examining the law during the progress of the trial he became convinced that it was a relic of barbarism and should be largely abolished. Governors Tilden and Robinson were men of national reputation, and their action gave prominence and historical significence to the case. It was a closely contested political struggle, in which entered the feeling between Utica and Rome. No man was more conspicuous in the case than ex-Sheriff David Moulton. He was bound to remove Benedict. It is said that party spirit ran high when Moulton was removed, and that for that reason Governor Seward was severe. When the eminent counsel D. M. K. Johnson saw politics were being dragged into the case, he remarked to the author that he "despised the man who was cowardly enough to sacrifice principle and manhood for political revenge." Yet how many men pay their debts and avenge their grievances in that way. In these things Oneida county has always been a great sufferer, and will be, so long as it is a halfshire county. Had such things not existed we believe Ellis H. Roberts would have been Governor of the State and Roscoe Conkling President of the nation.

FREDERICK G. WEAVER.

January 1, 1877, Frederick G. Weaver, son of the late Sheriff George F. Weaver, became Sheriff of the county. He brought to the office an experience as Deputy and the counsel and advice of his father. Being a man of good judgment and careful business habits, he soon became a model Sheriff. He was young and active, in fact the youngest man that ever held the office, being only 33 years of age. No deputy under him was allowed to do any important work without being first examined at the office in Utica. His brother, Van Rensselaer Weaver, was Undersheriff and the two did most of the work in person. Sheriff Weaver did all the important work himself, both civil and criminal. His first capital case was that of David White for murdering Solomon Christopher, in the town of Vernon, while engaged in a drunken altercation. White was convicted and imprisoned for life. Then followed the exciting Bush burglary in Main street, Utica. This was a grand piece of work, both on the part of the police and the Sheriff. Barnard McClusky and John Sheehan were arrested for the crime and in less than 10 days were safely in Auburn Prison. The Oyer and Terminer was in session, Judge George H. Harding presiding. A special Grand Jury was ordered and they were indicted and tried immediately. In this case an example was set worthy of precedent. Then followed the Deerfield burglaries, at Brown's and Budlong's. This was another well managed case. To catch the culprits, the Sheriff and his deputies had a lively chase over the Deerfield Hills and down its ravines. When the prisoners were overtaken, one was secured and the other took to the woods. He was fired upon by the Sheriff with the same revolver that shot Conroy, the bullet cutting through the shoulder of his heavy coat. He then threw up his hands and surrendered. They gave their names as Thomas Jacques and William

Alvord. In a short time they were landed in Auburn Prison.

THE GREAT RAILROAD RIOTS.

Then came the great railroad riots and insurrection. Cars were stopped and run off the tracks and the curious people assembled in large numbers. There were probably nearly a thousand tramps and strangers in the city and all along the different lines of road. Some were vicious, blood-thirsty Anarchists and bent on plunder and the destruction of property. They were principally strangers and were here principally to pilfer and to rob the unfortunates. The excitement grew so fierce and threatening that the city was declared in insurrection and marshal law enforced. The military was all under arms and special guards were organized for sentinel duty. The militia and veterans were ready to march at a moment's notice. These forces were all under the direction of the author by direction of the Sheriff and the Governor. Every available weapon was secured and put under guard or buried. When all things were in readiness, the author rode through the midst of the threatening elements, read his commission and the proclamation of the Governor and ordered them to disperse. The elements that were for fire and plunder, were bitter and disappointed, for the labor element took sides with the author for law and order. By good judgment a great catastrophe was avoided. At one time, when we were addressing the enraged people, we would not have given a $10 note for the fine residences of our railroad magnates and moneyed men. If a great fire and panic had occurred, it would have bankrupted the county, as all the railroads and other great corporations served notices, making the county liable and demanding protection. As it was, the cost was about $20,000. The county was bonded that year for $40,000. Some counties along the path of the great strikes in the West were bonded, foreclosed and ruined by insurrection. We mention this to show the necessity of having a good, reliable man for Sheriff. The riots were very much aggravated by the railroad authorities cutting down the wages of their employes and increasing their own salaries and profits.

THE LEADER ARRESTED.

The author put the leading striker under arrest, but released him at once upon hearing the following statement: "They have doubled their Superintendent's salary and reduced mine to 90 cents. I have earned $5 per day for the same work and skill. The superintendent got $1,000 and now gets $2,000 for the same work. There is no proof of any extra ability on his part and no additional duties. He was married the other day with great pomp and costly array. He wasted thousands in extravagance and vanity. My children were at school, well dressed and respected. Now they remain at home or go in poverty. Is this justice? Is this right? Is it American? I respect you and your official position, but have we no redress for our wrongs?" We ordered him to tack the proclamation of the Governor in a conspicious place before his co-workers and advise them all to go to their homes, pledging ourselves to do all in our power to correct the wrongs. On doing this and on their compliance, he was released. It would have been a horrible thing to have irritated them and then turned the guns of the military upon them. This was done in some places and a dreadful slaughter ensued. In Oneida county, decision, composed and calm judgment avoided any serious trouble. Out of these great strikes have arisen the great labor organizations. The reduction of wages was harsh and worked a great injustice. It came too suddenly and too severely, but it was the history of the world repeating itself—"Man's inhumanity to man, makes countless thousands mourn."

THE AUDITS.

When the Supervisors met there was a strong and exciting session. The bills presented by the military and other officers were large and many of them excessive. A combination was formed to secure their audit. Into this combination came Miles C. Comstock with a bill for about $1,300 for special services and disbursements in connection with the Germond burglary cases. This was referred to a special committee, with Jonathan Jones, of Utica, as Chairman. Members Crossett, of Sangerfield, and Townsley, of Vernon, Eames, of Lee and Grant, of Boonville, were his assistants. The first three members of the committee made a favorable report. It was to the effect that valuable services were performed, and in the discretion of the Board should be allowed.

By various manipulations a majority of the members of the Board were induced to vote for the adoption of the report and a draft was ordered. The county was bonded for this and other debts to avoid an increased levy of the tax that year. Jones and his committee were indicated by the Grand Jury for alleged misconduct in allowing Comstock's claim, but before a

trial could be had, Jones was taken sick and died.

The two latter made a minority report in which they said that the claim was unworthy of audit but the report was not accepted. For this action, however, they were not indicted.

Comstock's services, it was claimed were never authorized by the Sheriff or county officials. The committee found that the county was benefitted by his services and that his disbursements should be refunded.

BARN BURGLARS.

The Sheriff now turned his attention to the extermination of a gang of burglars in the Third Assembly District. Before he got through they were completely annihilated and about fifteen of them placed behind the bars at Auburn. Charles Rudd, Thomas Keats, James Manning, Michael Golden and John S. Kinney were among the number.

TEMPERANCE REVIVAL.

A great temperance revival now occurred under Frost, Evans and McKelvey. Public sentiment ran wild against the saloons and Excise Board of Utica. The Board and a large number of saloon keepers were indicted. This was the greatest crusade ever conducted against the liquor traffic in this county, and had it been followed up, would have resulted in great good. As it is, all that remains is a few reformed men.

DANFORD VS. WEAVER.

One of the most celebrated civil cases ever tried in Oneida county was that of Danford against Frederick G. Weaver as Sheriff. The Sheriff had arrested a well-known citizen who had settled a case in Surrogate's court improperly and in the interest of the widow and in opposition to some of the creditors. The matter was finally contested and decided against the man who had been arrested. It was a rather peculiar proceeding and full of sharp practice. The arrest was made on several attachments from Surrogate's court. Bonds were given for the prisoner for the liberties of the jail and both sureties died. Their estates were settled without notice of the liability. The wife of the prisoner was burned to death while her husband was on the limits. Forest Hill Cemetery is beyond the limits line, and the prisoner accompanied the family on the day of the funeral as far as the limit line and was about to get out of the carriage, when his children began to cry and plead with him to accompany them to the grave. He finally yielded to their tears and crossed the limit line.

A spy had followed the funeral with a horse and carriage in the line with the other carriages forming the solemn procession. When the limits were passed, suddenly the carriage wheeled out of the procession and sped back to the Sheriff's office with a Supreme writ to serve on that official. It was quickly served by the officer and the spy sped back to the line watch in hand, but the procession had re-crossed the limits. Another spy, however, had accompanied the cortege to the grave and returned with it and on his evidence, corroborated as it seemed to be, the jury found that the prisoner was beyond the line when the papers were served. This made the Sheriff liable for an escape and cost him nearly $3,000. The only remedy the Sheriff had was to arrest the prisoner when his bondsman or bondswoman died or burned to death and commit him to jail. Such action would have prevented his attending his wife's funeral and consoling his children. This seems to be the most damnable outrage ever perpetrated in the name of the civil law and of American jurisprudence. The case may be found in both the reports of the General Term and of the Court of Appeals. The author then swore vengeance on body executions as a relic of barbarism, and has fought his way to the Legislature year by year, till it is now so modified as to be almost worthless. He reported case after case in various matters until an investigation was ordered. There are a number of humane statues now on our books placed there through his influence and advice.

After citing this record it is almost useless to say that Mr. Weaver was a good Sheriff—the fact is, he was never excelled—and Oneida county may well be proud of Frederick G. and Van R. Weaver.

FRANCIS X. MEYERS.

January 1, 1880, Col. Francis X. Meyers, of Utica, succeeded Frederick G. Weaver. Previous to the war for the Union, he was a merchant and shoe dealer. When the war broke out, he raised a company and was made Captain of Co. C. 117th Regiment, N. Y. S. Volunteers. By meritorious service, he was successfully promoted through the grades to Lieutenant Colonel of the regiment. In the gallant charge on Fort Fisher, he so distinguished himself as to win the title of Colonel. A resolution of commendation and thanks was voted him by the Legislature of the State. He was a brave and popular soldier participating in all the battles of his regiment. At the capture of Fort Fisher he was badly wounded in the shoulder. In politics he was originally a Democrat, but from the time Sumpter's guns echoed the sound of war he was a Republican, loyal to the Union and true and faithful in all things.

The very large and flattering majority he received for Sheriff proved the appreciation of a grateful people. Before assuming the duties in the Sheriff's office he had failed in the furnishing goods business. This proved a great embarrassment to him in his term of office. He was, however, an eminently honest man and determined to pay all his debts to the full satisfaction of all his creditors. After starting on his official duties the first case to require his attention was that of James Welch, Jr., for killing a comrade while intoxicated at Oneida Castle.

JESSE SMITH AND MATTHEW FLANIGAN.

This was closely followed by the indictment of Jesse Smith and Matthew Flanigan for the murder of an old gentleman named Vedder at North Bay. The case was one of arsenical poisoning. Jesse was said to be a wayward girl. She ran the hotel for Vedder, who had been a Madison county farmer. In her younger days she was beautiful and bewitching but time and dissipation left marks on her countenance and once almost perfect features. The trial was long and tiresome and resulted in an acquittal. There were all sorts of rumors about the jury and their conclusion. Jesse is said to have been intimately acquainted with two or three of them and that they were very friendly to her cause. Her case decided Flanigan's. Poison was found in Vedder's system but no one could identify her with it or in its purcase.

WILLIAM HENRY OSTRANDER.

The next case was that of William Henry Ostrander for killing his brother at West Camden. He was an ignorant, dissipated and desperate fellow. The murdered brother lived in Connecticut and was home spending the holidays. They quarreled over taking one of the younger sisters to Connecticut. It was Sunday morning and they were preparing for church. William Henry had been drinking cider and was ugly and very offensive. Revolvers were drawn by each, which finally resulted in the fatal shot. He was convicted of murder in the first degree and sentenced to be hanged.

ANO STODDARD.

The next case was the murder of James Vanderpool by Ano Stoddard in West Utica. Stoddard had been doing the saloons and came home drunk. Vanderpool was a veteran of the late war and constable of the Ninth Ward. He was called in by Mrs. Stoddard to aid in quieting her husband. Stoddard flew into a passion and shot Vanderpool and mortally wounded him. He died in a few days. Stoddard was tried and convicted of manslaughter and sent to the penitentiary at bany.

MICHAEL ROCO.

Michael Roco was an Italian and shot and killed a fellow laborer at Cassville. They had been drinking and had an altercation about a woman who did their cooking. Roco escaped to Europe, sailing from New York to Paris. The Supervisors thought it best to let him stay there.

FERDINAND KOENIG.

Ferdinand Koenig, beat his wife until she died, while in a beastly state of intoxication. They were both in about the same condition. He was allowed to plead to manslaughter.

SALOON MURDER.

Then came the murder in a West Utica saloon for which John Brandt was arrested with several others. A drunken man was thrown from the building and so injured that he died. In this case there seems to have been no conviction.

MILTON D. BARNETT.

The bar of Oneida county will wait many a long day before it finds a young man who can excel in eloquence the late District Attorney Milton D. Barnett. He was a scholar, a fine orator and a brilliant advocate. For years while in official life, he rode with the advanced tide of public sentiment. He was the most popular man of his time and full of hope and promise. The people looked to him as the guardian of their most sacred rites. He had their full confidence and respect. But in an evil hour, when he had little thought an enemy was at the threshold of his very home with a concealed dagger for his heart, jealousy, envy, hatred and malignant falsehood, were following in his pathway. Exposed self-interest knows no bounds. The political defamer, like death, loves a shining mark. Such was the fate of Milton D. Barnett. He was indicted for receiving a bribe deposited with James C. Daly for his benefit to

quash the indictment against one Asa Jones. When the indictment was quashed Jones wanted his money back and Daly refused to give it up. If that was all there was in the case, Jones could have recovered his money bringing an action in the court. Had he done so and if Barnett had the money, it would have been refunded. But no, there were other influences in the case. Barnett swore he never received a cent of the money. We believe him. From a personal knowledge of some of the facts, we could not do otherwise. We took certain acknowledgements that would indicate that the money went in another way. On the great trial Barnett was acquitted but ruined. His prospects were blasted, his hopes were gone, his proud spirit was crushed and humbled in the dust. He had been suspected of crime, the loved ones that confided in him were abashed and humiliated. His wife and adopted boy were stung to the heart, their home was clouded with suspected infamy, the blow was too heavy; it was more than he could bear; it shattered his intellect; it grieved him; it sapped the vitals of life; death alone brought him relief. He welcomed it as a sweet harbor of repose. If there is anything cruel in this world of ours, it is such cases as this. Would that every newspaper and every scandalizer might realize this fact when they utter charges against their fellow men. There are innocent hearts that can be stung; there are those that suffer for others' wrongs. We have said this much because we have a knowledge of the facts and a firm conviction it is right and our love of justice demands it. It cannot help Milton D. Barnett; he is beyond the need of mortal aid, but we sincerely hope it may, to some extent, relieve the aching hearts and help drive the reproach from his memory. He was not faultless. He may have yielded to temptation in some things but whatever may be the fact, reader,

"Gently scan thy brother man,
Still gentler sister woman,
Though they may gang a heinous wrong,
To step aside is human."

And we are all human.

OTHER CASES.

There were other cases of importance—among them that of Henry Renshaw for a deadly assault on Dr. John P. Gray at his office in the New York State Lunatic Asylum. He was found insane and committed for treatment. Another was the killing of Johnny Martin by a jealous pal in the Fifth Ward, Utica, but the most shocking of all was the wicked and cruel operation by Dr. Thomas Spier, which caused the death of Mrs. George Lawrence. He was a low, misguided and drunken brute. One of those men of his profession who seek to make a living out of the misfortune of unhappy and conscience-less young women. Like all men of that character, he entertained low, vulgar ideas of human existence. Whisky was his idol and his God. He had taken too much, his hand was unsteady and he tore the very vitals from the poor woman's body. For this he was arrested and put under $10,000 bonds. He was indicted by the Grand Jury and a warrant issued when it was too late. The villian had escaped and forfeited his bail, which was paid to the County Treasurer. His escape was made on the Utica & Black River Railroad, in the darkness of the night. A spy and private detective accompanied him beyond the lines. Spier was wrapped in a great coat and feigned sleep. The private detective handed the conductor the tickets while sitting in the same seat, then changed his position to watch while the fleeing culprit slept. This is one of the cases where the secrets of the Grand Jury were divulged to the injury of the enforcement of civil law and justice. Every officer and juror should have been called into court and examined, so that the wrong-doer could have been punished.

RIOTS ON THE WEST SHORE.

During the last year of Col. Meyers' term a desperate riot occurred on the West Shore railroad. A band of Italians, about 200 strong, had gathered on the road, where they were laboring between the East county line and Westmoreland. They became dissatisfied with their pay and went on strike. Many of them became intoxicated and in their madness assembled their forces at Hampton and beyond. They took possession of the Brockett Brewery and drank to their fill. The people all along the line of march became alarmed and locked and barred their doors. Many depredations were committed. A dispatch was sent to the Sheriff, who, with the author repaired at once to the scene of action. A posse was summoned and an exciting battle ensued. The author caught the ring leader and put him under arrest. The entire band then opened the attack with knives, stilletos, clubs and stones. During this melee the leader escaped. The author ordered him to surrender. He refused and drew his knife. A more savage and desperate man

we never saw. As he lifted his arm to strike the author shot his knife into the air and put a ball through his hand. He then took to the woods in flight. Several shots were fired and several of the Italians were slightly wounded. A dark and heavy cloud hung directly over the contending forces. There was a clear, bright electric flash and a thunder clap as though all heaven's artillery had opened upon us, and it seemed as if the clouds had burst and the rain came down in torrents. This was a lucky thing for the Sheriff and the Italians retreated to an old factory near by and used them as a barracks or stopping place. No officer could have been put in a worse position. The Italians could not understand a word spoken and fought like desperate savages. An interpreter was called and entered the room and advised them to disperse. They now got to quarreling among themselves. The Sheriff reinforced his posse and the author went and directed the Italians to at once disperse and leave for their homes. As the posse prepared to advance upon them they retired. The wounded were taken to a doctor's and had their wounds dressed. This ended the strike, and all went to work but a few desperate leaders who fled from the penalties of the law.

Meyers was a kind hearted, upright and honest man, but failed to make as much money as some other Sheriffs.

ANECDOTES.

One day in the early part of the Colonel's term, a large attachment was received at the office to enforce against the property of Gen. James H. Ledlie, who was associated with the Colonel in the army. The General was an old Utica boy and came to this city from Nebraska to attend the funeral of his mother. He was superintendent of a Western railroad. Not thinking of the sharp scheme being worked upon him, he deposited $12,000 in the First National Bank. The money was attached by the author for a New York firm. After the funeral the General went to draw his money to return home and was advised of the attachment. This frustrated all his plans, and for the world he would not let his corporation know of it. He went to New York and arranged to settle. His arrangements were all perfected but Sheriff's fees and disbursements which amounted to about $400. The General and the Sheriff talked about war times and their friendly relations while before Petersburg and the various other struggles in life. Finally the General told of his trials and afflictions and asked the Colonel to take $100 The author stepped up and told the Sheriff he would wait many a long day before he got another such a fee. The Colonel responded, when he told me of his troubles and the old war associations and the hardship it would work: "I haven't the heart to take any more".

On another occasion a large execution was received against Gen. James G. Grindley. The Colonel was instructed to go to his house and make a levy. The Colonel went to the General and told him of his troubles and the cause of his embarrassment. They chatted of old times and the changes of business and its disappointments. The General agr ed to pay it as fast as he could. The Colonel left without making a levy. The author asked him if he had levied. He said he had not the heart to do it. It looked like a breach of confidence of a friend in friend. "In war times I would trust him with my life, and I will trust him now. I can't do it." So the author had to go and make the levy. These things look harsh, but they have to be done and done right. If the levy had not been made in this case just when it was, the Sheriff would have been liable for the entire amount of the judgment as other creditors were awaiting their claims. No Sheriff can legally show charity until he secures himself and his processes.

The Colonel was a brave and kindhearted man. Had he been County Clerk instead of Sheriff, he could have saved a fortune. His heart was too big for the severe duties of Sheriff if he wanted to make money. Few nobler men live today. As it was the business was all done in the best possible manner, but with small fees and malice toward none and charity for all. Spriggs & Mathews were his counsel and legal advisers in all that pertained to his office. The Colonel ought to be rich in friends if not in this world's goods. He is naturally honest, upright and deserving.

THOMAS D PENFIELD.

In the great and stirring campaign of 1882, there was a general revolution in the politics of Oneida county. Only one Republican was elected and that was County Clerk and he was snatched as a brand from the burning. The State also went Democratic by an overwhelming majority. Grover Cleveland, an old Oneida county boy, was elected Governor over that eminent scholar, jurist and statesman,

Charles J. Folger. And the ambitious and crafty politician, David B. Hill, was elected Lieutenant Governor by the greatest majority of them all. This was a campaign of hatred, bitterness and revenge. Principle, manhood, integrity and worth were all sacrificed on the altar of political vengeance. Spite triumphed over right; political greed over gratitude and justice. The *Utica Morning Herald* had supported the citizen's (Democratic) candidate for Mayor in the city election in the spring and omitted the names of the party in the general election in the fall. Its friends and its foes all went to the wall together and foreshadowed the defeat of their Presidential candidate in 1884, James G. Blaine. Conkling and Platt had resigned from the United States Senate, the lamented Garfield had been murdered, and Chester A. Arthur was President of the nation. The Republican party in the county of Oneida was in a state of political chaos. But, fortunately for the people, the Democracy nominated for Sheriff one of their most esteemed and venerable leaders, Thomas D. Penfield, of Camden. He was born and raised in the county and was a native of the town. The ruins of a little old log cabin on the hillside about two miles from the village of Camden, marks the spot of his birth. What remains is now covered by the fragrant wild flower and delicate ferns while the woodvine twines around the decaying posts and sleepers. It is a lovely spot and a fit reminder of younger days. No wonder his eyes are dimmed with tears as he recalls its grateful remembrances. Here he played in childhood and loves to linger still. Here was father; here was mother; here were the sweet and lasting impressions of youthful days. Here the heroic manhood was developed for the life of usefulness that followed. From here he moved to the village to learn the boot and shoe trade before he reached his majority, and in the village he has resided ever since. Its improvements and advancements have been his greatest pride and pleasure. He has honored the village and the village has honored him To write the complete history of the one, would almost be the history of the other. He was born November 22, 1813—nearly 77 years ago. His father was a Connecticut farmer and settled on the homestead (Camden) farm, where Thomas was born in the early days of the century. He was married to the mother of the subject of our sketch in 1807. In those days the young boys were fortunate who could enjoy the benefits and the privileges of the district schools. They alone furnished the education of many of our greatest and most eminent men. Such alone were the opportunities and the privileges of Thomas D. Penfield. After learning his trade, he followed it as an occupation for many years, and by industry and skill, succeeded in amassing an independent fortune and building a fine residence and shop. He now sought to invest his earnings in other business avocations for the benefit of the village. In 1854, he purchased of the late Sheriff, Gen. Lyman Curtis, all his right, title and interest in the flouring and grist mills. He now became a partner of that successful business man. F. H. Conant, who also owned an interest in the mills. On this property is located the elegant stone mansion of Sheriff Lyman Curtis, now owned by Sheriff Penfield. Two years later, Mr. Conant sold his interest to Thomas Stone, a brother-in law of Mr. Penfield. The firm continued in business until the death of Mr. Stone, in 1861. A few years later, his son, Hon. Benjamin D. Stone, became and ever since has been a partner of Mr. Penfield in the mill business.

Mr. Penfield is one of the very few men who have actively engaged in politics and successfully managed a large private business. From a poor, honest and industrious boy, he has become a wealthy business man and great land owner. In politics he has always been an ardent and consistent Democrat. His public life was inaugurated as School Commissioner in 1842. He next served as Justice of the Peace and as Justice for the Oneida County General Sessions. For 11 terms he has represented his town in the Board of Supervisors, his first term was in 1851 and his last in 1886. In 1856 he was duly elected to the State Assembly as a Democrat, and again in 1862. He was a war Democrat and stood for the Union and for the freedom of the down-trodden and oppressed. Be it said to his great credit, that he voted to maintain the war policy of President Abraham Lincoln, and in advocating such a course, stood alone among the members of his party. Some of them reproached him and assailed him with taunts and sneers. But no scoffs, no taunts, abuse or jeers could move him from his conviction of duty. He was for his country; he was for a united nation and stood up to be counted for the Union every time and for the abolition of human slavery.

This will ever stand among other noble deeds as a monument of glory and the proudest monument erected to his memory. On the second ballot and final passage of the act, 11 other Democrats came over and voted with him and the loyal Republicans.

It takes a brave man to break away from a party under such circumstances. But such was the act of Thomas D. Penfield. Recall the exciting times: The war cloud; the approaching enemy; the threatened invasion of the North; the terrible suffering; the half mounted flags; the defeats of our army; the discouragements; the blood and tears, and it needs no comment. Words are far too feeble to give expression to the grandeur of the thought. There was weeping at almost every fireside and in many homes a vacant chair; our churches and our schools were draped in mourning and our land was drenched with blood. The sound of chiming bells and marshal music floated in mingled, yet mournful harmony upon every breeze. Vicksburg had not fallen; Gettysburg had not been fought, yet the voice of Penfield was for the Union. In 1879, he was for the fourth time elected to the Assembly and again did himself and constituents great credit. Governor Robinson spoke of him as the man who always voted on the right side. For years he has been prominent in the county affairs of Oneida and its religious, agricultural, mercantile and manufacturing industries. As a member of the agricultural society, he has many times been honored as its President and as a member of its executive committee. He has been nine times President of the village, served as Water Commissioner and several times as Commissioner of Highways for the town, as well as almost every other local office.

In 1872, Mr. Penfield was nominated for Congress by the Democratic Convention, with the assurance of election, but he refused. The Conkling wing of the Republican party had guaranteed their support as well as had the Liberals. Scott Lord was finally nominated and elected. He was a law partner of Hon. Roscoe Conkling. This was the beginning of the open war of the factions and resulted in the defeat of Congressman, Hon. Ellis H. Roberts In this year the Prohibition party had a full ticket in the field, Dr. R. E. Sutton ran for Congress. In 1879, he was a member of the Board of Equalization, and with Harvey Head, of Paris, and with Col. Pierce, of Bridgewater, visited every town in the county to properly adjust all matters of difference between city and towns. It is said that if their report had been lived up to, no further trouble need have occurred. He duly qualified as Sheriff January 1, 1883, and entered upon the discharge of his duties. The author's time then expired and he resolved to retire from public life. While seeking other avocations Sheriff Penfield sought his services and his counsel and engaged him for his term. And, though differing many times in politics, our personal relations were most pleasant, agreeable and profitable. Penfield was a high-minded citizen and prudent Chistian gentleman. Being such, he could not fail to make a most excellent Sheriff.

The first great capital case that came up under his admistration was one of homicide at Vienna.

LYDIA SCOVILLE.

Lydia Scoville was charged with taking the life of her own infant child. She was the victim of fraud and deceit and the low, vulgar passions of a vile and inhuman monster. The story of her ruin, downfall and disgrace is a sad one. Robbed of her innocence, the pride of her home, she was turned into the world friendless and unsheltered and left with her illegitimate offspring to wander and die. No one would employ her with her child. She groped in the darkness with her starving babe upon her breast, mourning and weeping until reason was dethroned, and then despairing of aid and relief, she stayed the breathing of her innocent and sleeping babe and buried it beneath the moss and laurel near a weeping willow. When charged with the crime she truthfully told the story of her wrong and the crime, and her plea of manslaughter was accepted by the District Attorney and the court. The kind-hearted and generous Sheriff pleaded for her life, and when she was sentenced went with her to plead with the keeper of the penitentiary for her proper care and protection. His influence was her noblest shield; his love of justice her greatest benefactor.

BLEECKER STREET TROUBLE.

In the early part of Penfield's term came the Bleecker Street Railroad trouble. Out of this has grown some very expensive and tedious litigation. Injunctions were granted and openly violated. Papers were served and disobeyed. Several arrests were finally made for misconduct while tearing up railroad ties and rails. The corporation served notice on the Sheriff to make the county liable. This necessitated a guard which cost the county several hundred dollars. After much delay and diplomacy, the matter was agreeably settled.

CAPITAL CRIMES.

The murder of John Hughes at the State Asylum by James Brown and Franklin Bills, by crushing his side and back while endeavoring to remove him from a chair came on for trial at Utica. Brown was convicted and fined $1,000. Then came the arrest of Michael Boylan for murder at Rome. He and a young man named Spellicy had been doing the saloons and finally got into a drunken altercation and Boylan fought and stabbed Spellicy near the heart. Poor Spellicy wandered away and died in the street. Then followed the most dreadful and shocking murder of Theresa Johnson by Calvin McHarg at Forestport. Having made an attempt to violate her person and failed, McHarg turned and shot her down like a dog. He was convicted of murder in the second degree and imprisoned for life. McHarg was a low, lecherous and craving libertine and deserved his fate. His case was hardly disposed of when John and Michael Funnell were indicted for killing Joseph Parette while desecrating the Sabbath in a drunken carousal. John was convicted and sentenced for life. Michael escaped to Italy. The next case placed upon the calendar was that of a Chinaman at Rome.

FONG AH YU.

His name was Fong Ah Yu. He killed a fellow Chinaman in a laundry at Rome. Pretending friendship he soon obtained the confidence of his victim, and while enjoying his hospitality, and steeping by his side upon his couch, drove a dagger to his heart. It was the coolest piece of villiany and murder that was ever perpetrated in Oneida county. The case was handled with great skill and ability on the part of the people and defense. The prisoner escaped to Canada but was extradited, tried and imprisoned for life.

JOSIAH PERRY.

The defense of this coldhearted and senseless Mongolian was conducted by Josiah Perry, of Utica, and had it not been for his skill in advocacy and pathetic appeal to the jury, the Sheriff would have undoubtedly cracked his neck and put an end to his miserable existence. In the midst of his argument, Perry grew very eloquent in speaking of the wayward wanderer, the homeless, friendless, unsheltered victim of prejudice and alien rage; away from home and kindred, with no one to counsel or render sympathy in his misfortune. The defense was an alibi and that another might have done the foul deed. On this theory Perry, by his eloquence, fairly begged him off and saved his life. The jury was composed of kindhearted, Christian men, and some of them during the trial grew weary of the thought of capital punishment. In these days of unsullied public sentiment juries are more apt to be lenient than ever.

WILLIAM HENRY OSTRANDER.

The case of William Henry Ostrander was confirmed in all things by the Court of Appeals. He was, accordingly, resentenced to be hanged, by the judges of the Supreme Court. He was finally executed by Sheriff Penfield at the old jail in Utica in August, 1883. Before he was hung, a committee on lunacy was appointed, who declared him sane. No one who attended, the execution would have much confidence in their opinions. He cursed and swore at the audience, even while prayer was being offered, and on the very threshold of death. The Sheriff did his duty and did it well, under very trying circumstances.

W. A. MATTESON.

During most of Penfield's term, W. A. Matteson was District Attorney, and, though a Republican, everything passed harmoniously and the criminals feared and trembled. Matteson was a man of good judgement and a very successful prosecuting officer. So has been his successor, Hon. Thomas S. Jones. The police forces in Utica and Rome have also been greatly improved.

THE NEW JAILS.

The new jails at Utica and Rome were completed during Sheriff Penfield's term and were duly occupied by his jailors. They are models of architecture, safety and convenience. In connection with the jail at Utica there is a workhouse for breaking stone. The scheme was first advocated by the late John F. Seymour as a humane enterprise to keep the prisoners from vice and the school of evil, taught by the vicious in the prison. Sheriff Penfield made a dignified and successful officer. He believed in running all the courts and making appointments that would command public esteem and respect. He is yet living to enjoy the fruits of his labors at his beautiful home in Camden.

THE OLD GRIST MILL

A peculiar instance occurs in the Sheriffs' record about the old mill at Camden. Gen. Curtis, who was Sheriff from that town, owned the grist mill now owned and run by Thomas D. Penfield. Sheriff Curtis sold it to Sheriff Penfield. In the history of that old mill is a grand biographical sketch of the two Sheriffs, and quite a little of the political history of the town of Camden. Nearby stands the old stone mansion of the General. Some day the author hopes to be able to give some very interesting reminiscences of these historical spots, when writing of the good men and true of Oneida county.

JOHN BATCHELOR.

In that most exciting of all campaigns of 1884, Grover Cleveland was elected President of the United States over the Plumed Knight of Republican leadership, James G. Blaine. Oneida county, for the first time in more than three decades gave a majority for the Presidential candidate of the Democracy. The friends of that stalwart leader, Hon. Roscoe Conkling, became the avengers of their tried and ever loyal companion, Charles J. Folger. Under their war cry the Republican standard was furled away for another battle. Blaine, with all his brilliant greatness, could not marshal them for his cause. They never ceased their toil, they never tired of the work until the wires flashed the news of his defeat, and then they claimed the battle as their own. But is it true? We often thought so, until we read the published statement that Hon. John B. Finch, a Prohibitionist leader, was the Blucher in this modern Waterloo. His bosom friend in the published statements of that canvas makes him the promulgator of "Rum, Romanism and Rebellion." He took and verified the steno graphic notes that so electrified the world Manning and Finch were bosom friends and often worked and roomed together * Both were originally Democrats, and both have now gone to their final rest. But whatever may have been the real fact the Republicans were badly disorganized in Oneida county. In the fall of 1885, they met in convention and nominated to lead the ticket for Sheriff John Batchelor of Utica. He was a native of the city and a son and partner of the great agriculturist, Daniel Batchelor, of the Farmers' Club. For years their store on the corner of Hotel and Liberty streets had been

*See *International Good Templar*, of London, Canada

the political headquarters of the tillers of the soil. Daniel, like the biblical hero after whom he was named, was a Stalwart among Stalwarts, and would rather face the lion in his den than surrender the smallest mite of his admiration for the pure and spotless banner of Roscoe Conkling. John was for the party every time and was bound to lead it on to victory. Together they made a powerful factor in its reorganization. The office must be redeemed by the Republicans. And it was redeemed. Previous to his election, Sheriff Batchelor had held several positions under the national and municipal government. He was their Supervisor from the Fourth Ward of the city. January 1, 1886, he duly qualified and entered upon the discharge of his duties, and served through three very trying and exciting years. The record shows an unparalelled amount of crime in capital cases. From beginning to end there was murder, blood and tears. He has since acted as Undersheriff under Sheriff Wheeler.

JOHN BENDER.

The first capital case under his care was that of John Bender. Bender was interested in a hotel in Deerfield, just across the bridge from Utica. Thomas Gray was interested in what was known as the old American in Utica. They had disagreed on several occasions. Unexpectedly, one evening, they met at the entrance of a place on Broad street. Then came a war of words, a fight, and finally Bender shot and killed Gray. At the time of the murder public sentiment was all in favor of Gray. Bender was convicted of murder in the second degree and imprisoned for life. Since the trial many who saw the battle and the shooting think the sentence was too severe. But the jury found in that degree, and that must end it until changed by appeal or commutation.

CHAEL ROARK.

The trial of Chael Roark for express robbery and gagging and shooting one Charles Leak, on the West Shore Railroad, was one of the most difficult ever brought before the courts of the county. No pains or money were spared to convict the offender. The management on the part of the District Attorney, detectives and officers, was marvelous and faultless. The matching of torn bills, pieces of sealing wax, strings, footmarks, identification of tones of voice and the establishment of other evidence of guilt were very skillful and exquisite. By this means the evidence was wound so tightly around

the prisoner that he was convicted and given the longest term for the crime. He was said to be a desperate man and had been identified with other crimes in the far West. He was a powerful man, one of the Jesse James stamp, full of exploit and daring.

CLEMENT ARTHUR DAY.

The next case was the indictment and trial of Clement Arthur Day for the murder of Joan M. Rosa, near Boonville, July 9, 1887. Joan was once a beautiful and lovely girl, well educated and scholarly. She had a natural taste and talent for music. In this respect she is said to have been brilliant. The home of a widowed mother was made happy by her presence. It was near Oneida Lake in the town of Vienna. She was fond of the beautiful in nature and art. Her mother attended to the home duties while she taught music. In her charming presence that rural home was bright and happy. But in the midst of all this joy and gladness the destroyer came and the little paradise on earth was made a hell. An officer of the law, yet a defamer of his own home, a despoiler of virtue, entered this blissful Eden and plucked the fairest of flowers. His breath was poison, his hand polluted all it touched. He crushed a mother's heart, he blasted the fair prospects of her promising child. This vile seducer, when he had accomplished his hellish work, turned coldly away and left her in her shame. Day found her in her sorrow and despair and spoke consoling words. He promised to care for her in her misfortune. They became attached but poverty stared them in the face. Day, too, was fond of music and delighted in the harp and violin, but he was jealous, low and cunning. They strayed away from home, further and further into the world. They became wearied and lay down, like tired children, to rest where night overtook them. Fate at last brought them to a poor hovel on the banks of the Black River Canal near Boonville. Is it a wonder that in this condition poor "Rosa" longed for home, though it were ever so humble? Is it surprising she reached out the hand for a friend in this condition of poverty and want? She longed for mother; she sighed for some one to whisper words of kindness and affection to her. Her mother had sent a message to her to come. Day despaired of her return and opposed her going. She started to go and in a fit of anger he drove the cruel dagger to her heart. He claimed her as his idol yet he slew her. He claimed he loved her, but it was the love of a low vulgar heart. Such love is the gall of bitterness to the pure soul. It seeks alone the gratification of the passions, it feeds on lust. Such a being pollutes and mildews everything it comes in contact with, and the sooner he is banished from the good and pure, the better for society, the better for the world. The law destroys such to save the good and virtuous from their wrath and destructive influence. Would that this lesson might be taught to all who seek to make a farce of the law when dealing with the institutions where congregate the slayers of the body and the soul; public defamers who despise heaven and blaspheme God.

Clement Arthur Day was a graduate of such schools of vice. He confessed his error when it was too late, and wept in anguish, but all his tears could not wipe the stain from his polluted heart. Yet society in permitting these things to exist, is more to blame than he. Had he not been surrounded by such influences he would have been a better man At last the crime ripened into murder and the penalty was death. He was executed at Utica by Sheriff Batchelor according to his sentence. In his last moments he sighed for a better life, he longed for forgiveness. But his final destiny is in the hands of Him,

"Who made the heart; 'tis He alone
Decidedly can try us.
He knows each care—its various tone,
Each Spring its various bias.
Then at the balance let's be mute,
We never can adjust it.
What's done we but partly can compute,
And know not what resisted."

CEDAR JOHN.

The next murder was that of "Cedar" John, or John Kenline, at Stittville, July 16, 1887. This was another unfortunate affair. Happy John had one failing, and that was love for the intoxicating cup. He came home from work on the evening of the murder deranged by its influence. He was truthfully "paralyzed." This has become a vulgar phrase, yet it is the truth. He found his tenement occupied by one Frederick Lipe. They had been friends, but whiskey, John's great foe, made enemies of the pair. The little hut, so often filled with frivolity and song, became the scene of a ghastly murder. They quarreled and Fred grabbed the fatal ax and struck the fatal blow. To-day he languishes in States prison at Auburn.

JOHN MINING AND OTHERS.

Another indictment for murder was that of John Mining There were also a large number of other cases of less de-

grees, a full mention of which would fill a large volume. King Alcohol seems to have been the vital cause and champion slayer of mankind. Lorenzo Marchitto made a slaughter house of a saloon in West Utica. There are some cases yet untried and it would be unfair to mention them until their history is complete.

VIRGIL JACKSON.

Now we come to the celebrated case of Virgil Jackson for killing Norton Metcalf, at Augusta, January 13, 1888. He was indicted for murder, tried and convicted and sentenced to be hanged at the new jail in Utica. An appeal was taken and a stay granted. Jackson was an educated man, a fine vocalist and fair musician, the popular singer in a church choir. He was the heir to a large fortune, the good influences of a Christian home. His prospects for a useful and promising life were the very best. But he entertained low and vulgar ideas of moral responsibility. He loved to be with those who congregate in public places for mirth and vulgar pleasure. In his weakness he yielded to temptation and fell. He sacrificed home, a wife's love, the tender affection of his children, his fortune, his honor, his manhood, his Christian influences, all for lust and the gratification of his passion. He became a bold and lecherous libertine, a heartless murderer. In his cravings he betrayed his wife and crept skulkingly into the home of his friend to lead a life of infamy and shame with the idol of that friend's heart. He became so loathsome and vile everything virtuous and pure fled from his polluted presence. He was so hardened in his crime of adultery that he followed his victim to the very sanctuary of God, and blasphemed at the very altar of repentance. From that place of worship he followed the object of his desire to the very threshold of her husband's protection where it was supposed they might dwell in safety and repose, crowned with virtue and with honor. But there was no repose; there was no protection from the lustful and murderous longings of this vile monster of human depravity. While the church bells were yet ringing out their notes of warning, while the Sabbath sun was brightly shining in the clear, blue sky, and all of mankind seemed to be enjoying the peaceful quietude of the sacred day, Jackson broke the stillness of the hour by coarse words, a shot and the cry of murder. Poor Metcalf, seeing his wife in such hands, met her at the gate of his own home, he rebukes them in the name of honor and

:be purity of his household and is slain. Such is the story of this crime.

The Court of Appeals confirmed the de decision of the Court below and Jackson was hung by Sheriff Wheeler March 14, 1890, at the new jail in Utica. This will probably be the last execution in Oneida county as all prisoners are now taken to Auburn S*ates Prison for imprisonment and for execution.

THE RAILROAD WAR.

One of the most novel affairs in the history of the Sheriff's office was that of the contending railroad forces of the Delaware, Lackawana & Western Company and the Ontario & Western Company against those of The Utica City Belt Line Street Railroad Company. We had passed through many similar scenes when outside parties were the aggressors, but here was a fight between railroads and street railroad corporations warring among themselves. The greater combining and trying to crush the lesser, each with their learned counsel and legal advisors. In order to enjoy the full benefit of the franchises, the Belt Line must cross the Delaware and Ontario. The work was completed, except the laying of the rails between the tracks of the great corporations. New and much needed enterprises were fast springing up in the western part of the city near the Eureka Mower Works. These people the Belt Line desired to accommodate. Their tracks must be completed, they must cross the other roads. They were laid down by the Belt Line and torn up by the workmen of the other roads. This was repeated time and again until the people became indignant and enraged. Papers were served upon the Sheriff, making the county liable for any destruction of property. Each and every corporation claimed superior rights to the other. The attorney of each had looked up the law and knew he was right. Had we been obliged to rely upon their advice the county would have been the sufferer, but the discipline secured under that old railroad champion, D. Minor K. Johnson, now came into play, and our own experience fully prepared us for the event and the occasion. On the start the Ontario and the Delaware had the advantage of an operated road. They had engines, cars, men and the right of way But they lacked tact, skill, diplomacy, and good judgment. They relied too much on brute force, and in that way enraged the people against them. As the Belt Line men laid the necessary tracks

they removed them, and an engine fitted for the occasion was worked to prevent their being relaid.

But the Belt Line again watched their opportunity and their men laid them down again. A band of men was brought by special train and again tore them up. But again they were relaid, and this time Treasurer Charles W. Mather planted his horse and carriage in front of the hideous looking engine and bade them defiance. Under the d rection of their counsel the railroad was now put in active operation, and as car after car passed, the assembled multitude grew wild with applause and enthusiastic cheers The Sheriff and his deputies must now do their duty and arrest all persons interfering with the property so as to endanger the traveling public. The rights of the innocent must be protected. There was great excitement for several days and much confusion. Some of the workmen let their angry passions rise and were arrested. Finally in their calm movements the representatives of the great corporations met and mutually settled their differences, leaving the Belt Line in full possession of all their corporative rights. Perhaps no railroad corporation has had more impediments thrown in its way than the enterprising and thrifty Belt Line of our city. In their efforts to perfect their road and render good service to the people they have been fre quently obstructed by those who love to indulge in the luxury of a law suit. Action after action has been commenced to restrain them from proceeding with their improvements to keep up with the neces sity of the times. Injunction after injunc tion has been served and the Sheriff called upon to enforce the mandates of the courts. But in almost every case it has come out victorious, and in most every instance the ir junctions have finally been dissolved and set aside. So at last we glide along in the electric coach, the present pride and delight of the city. In all these legal triumphs their young attorney, John W. Boyle, has shown great tact, professional skill and good judgment and diplo macy. He has well earned the success that has crowned his efforts. The Sheriff has had to walk the line of duty, protecting the rights of all and guarding with a zealous care the interests of the sovereign people.

John Batchelor, being a prompt and energetic business man, succeeded well as Sheriff. He was prudent, economical and industrious, and now enjoys the benefits of a beautiful and pleasant home on Rutger street, in his native city. He is one of the most genial and affable men we were ever associated with, and we sincerely hope he may live long to enjoy the fruits and honors of his successful official labor. His term was full of trying cases and many important criminal and civil causes, which often called for discretion, skill, ability and a nerve of iron. He was ever equal to the task, and his efforts have been crowned with success. For some reason during his term there seemed to be an unusual amount of crime. From the record we draw these conclusions: Increased population and looseness in the license laws. The low places, where many of the crimes are committed and which some times come into the hands of the Sheriff by virtue of civil processes, are dirty haunts of vice and disease, unwholesome pests in the community, fit subjects for the investigation of the Health Officer and his inspectors.

THOMAS WHEELER.

The year one thousand, eighteen hundred and eighty-eight was a Presidential year, and many indeed were the candidates for the office of Sheriff. Both parties were anxious and determined to elect their whole ticket. The Democrats had the advantage of the national patronage. Strong men were sought for with a large personal following. After balloting for hours the Republicans nominated Thomas Wheeler of Utica. This was the soldiers' campaign. Benjamin, Harrison, their candidate for President was a soldier. Warner Miller, who ran for Governor, was a soldier and Thomas Wheeler was a soldier. The influence of the Southern Democracy in the Democratic caucus had alarmed the sturdy veterans of the late war so they rallied around the standard of General Harrison. No organization in the whole campaign had a greater influence on the voters than the veteran Forty Rounders. The canvas was brilliant and successful. Oneida county went overwhelmingly Republican. Wheeler's majority was the largest ever given to any candidate for Sheriff, aggregating over 4,000. Prior to his election he had been policeman, deputy sheriff and county detective. He had also held several positions under the municipal government of Utica, among them Health Commissioner and Inspector. For many years he was in the employ of the New York Central and Hudson River Railroad Company, as special detective and police officer. In all these positions he had won an enviable reputation as a competent and efficient official. Perhaps there is not a better organizer in the State. When he makes a friend he holds him and puts him in line. This is done by keeping his word and never betraying a friend or trust.

HIS WAR RECORD.

In 1862, at the age of 16 years, he enlisted in Col. Joseph S. Lowery's Co. C, 146th Regiment, New York State Volunteers. This regiment was called the Fifth Oneida and was one of the finest military organizations in the Army of the Potomac. Shortly after their arrival at the front in December, 1862, they were marched directly to the battle of Fredericksburg, and were at Chancellorville, Gettysburg and almost all the great battles of Grant's campaign from the Wilderness to the surrender of Lee at Appamatox Court House. They were a fighting regiment and early in their history were reinforced by the three years' veterans of Gen. James McQuade's old 14th, the First Oneida and those of the gallant 44th and from other sources. Their history is full of glowing and meritorious service. Being in the old 5th Army Corps, they were as well disciplined and marched with the precision of regulars. The record of Thomas Wheeler is closely identified with that of the gallant 146th. From a boy private of sixteen years, he was successively promoted until he came home at the close of the war, a Lieutenant in command of his company. Here is where he got in the tide that flows on to fortune. He was kind and generous with his command and his command were grateful and generous in the time of need. In his canvas they stood by him with their votes, lead by their commander, Gen. James G. Grindley. Lowery and Grindley were both Democrats, but they were both for Wheeler.

HIS CANVAS.

After coming home from the army, Wheeler made some mistakes and committed some grave errors which were the subject of a vigorous attack in his canvas for Sheriff. But being a frank and openhearted man, instead of trying to hide his faults and cover up the unfortunate things done in thoughtless moments of temptation, he appeared before the people and frankly admitted his mistakes and expressed a deep regret He promised, if elected, a faithful performance of duty without oppression, fear or reward. The people took him at his word and expressed their confidence in the overwhelming majority given. His competitor was also a brave Virginian and soldier of the Union army, Dr R. E. Sutton, of Rome. His name is identified with many of the most benevolent enterprises of Oneida county, his adopted home. In the great battles of temperance he is one of the most famous and gifted leaders. In this field of labor he has a world wide reputation and has often been crowned with successful official honors. He is a Past Grand Templar of the Order of Good Templars, an organization founded in Oneida county, and which has grown to adorn and bless the world. The unfortunate and ill advised attack on Sheriff Wheeler was against his wishes and without his consent. It was the worst piece of political buffoonery we ever heard of and did him great injustice. By its reaction the great and popular heart of the people was touched and the sympathetic hordes stampeded against him, to the ranks of his competitor.

IN OFFICE.

In the canvas Sheriff Wheeler promised the people a faithful discharge of his duty, and no man feels more sensitive about fulfilling a promise. We have been retained by him as counsel and have full control of all civil and legal matters, and in no case has he shrunk from the performance of any duty. Not a single instance can yet be recorded where his action has been disapproved by the courts. He has dared to do what others shrank from doing in the improvement of county buildings. The Sheriff's office was little more comfortable than an old barn. He has repaired, rearranged and refitted it, so that now it is a credit to our great and prosperous county. Some of the court rooms were rickety and unhealthful. He has made them cheerful and pleasant. The jails were out of repair in many things; he has made them wholesome and homelike. In doing this work and making needed repairs his efforts were seconded and aided by the taste and tact of county committeeman, Hon. John Buckley, of the Board of Supervisors. Not like some official, with a fear of reduction in his own bills, but with a personal responsibility and promise to make good anything ordered that did not meet with the approval of the courts and Board of Supervisors, many bills were paid from his own pocket. But the work was a work of necessity and met with the grateful recognition of both the courts and the board. It was for humanity's and others' comfort, not his own. He took the risk of having his own bills cut, a feature much dreaded by some others. Oneida county may now feel proud of the condition of its public buildings.

THE EXECUTION OF JACKSON.

One of the first and most painful of his duties was the hanging of Virgil Jackson for murder. It was one of the most quiet executions ever witnessed in Oneida county. No persons were allowed to witness it out of morbid curiosity. The officials and attendants required by law only were present. Such being the case everything passed off without flaw or commotion. The wishes and feelings of the prisoner were carefully considered and nothing done to irritate or annoy him. Most solemn indeed was the occasion. Jackson was in full possession of all his faculties. His mind was clear and he fully comprehended the situation. He listened with calm composure to the reading of the death warrant and marched to the scaffold more like a military chief than a man condemned to die. Yet he fully realized his terrible fate. It was sad to see such a promising man fall the victim of his vile passions and reap the death penalty. As he passed to the goal of death, he cast his eyes heavenward to behold the great light of day shining in all his splendor. He spoke of his beauties and the pleasant features of the day. Then, taking his position on the platform, he listened to the solemn prayer to the Great Father of all for mercy and forgiveness, and in the almost breathless silence that followed, he whispered an adieux to those he saw in his presence. He was then pinioned, veiled, the drop fell and his spirit was sent out in the realms of a vast eternity. He was gone from the world and gone forever, perhaps, as he thought, to a state of superior development, and perhaps to everlasting condemnation. His life on earth was wasted and in death he was poor indeed. Nearly all his friends forsook him and ruin claimed him as her own. Not even a tomb awaited his remains. His ashes, like his soul, were condemned and refused admission to the consecrated ground in our cemetery. Finally they were deposited by a kind and forgiving sister in a peaceful rural grove to await the awakening of the judgment day.

OTHER CASES.

During Sheriff Wheeler's term thus far, there have been few capital cases and among them is the Cibo murder case at Rome. Cibo is an Italian, and shot and killed one Gilson, while attempting to force his (Cibo's) door in a state of intoxication. The language used was so offensive as to enrage Cibo and his family. He thought his life in danger and shot and killed the offender. There have been very few felonies, among them the Burton incest, the Crandall malpractice and the Hampton burglaries; also some important cases of misdemeanor, among them the great frauds on the Prudential Life Insurance Company by Alexander Laski and his accomplices. But on the whole, crimes of the higher grades have diminished. There have been many misdemeanors of less degrees and the jails and penitentiaries are kept well filled with common drunks and tramps—about one and the same thing. Wipe out this class of criminals and Oneida county would be quite free from crime.

CIVIL CASES.

Among the great civil cases were those arising from the sale of the property of George Clarke. There were grave questions as to the rights of the respective creditors, and it became necessary to get an order of direction from the court as to the distribution of the surplus monies. Finally these were all settled without embarrassment to the Sheriff, and apparently with satisfaction to all parties interested. The distribution of this vast estate probably wipes out the last remnant of the feudal system in the Empire State. Clark seems to have inherited it from his ancestors and they from the British government.

LOUIS WINEBURG.

The case of Louis Wineburg is a novel one. Louis was a jeweler doing business in the old Grannis' Bank building. He failed and executions were placed in the Sheriff's hands. That official made a levy, an inventory was taken, and the property advertised for sale. But before the day of sale parties appeard from New York, and through Coroner Herbert G. Jones, seek to replevin some of the goods. No personal demand is made on the Sheriff or owner of the building. They attempt to talk with the Sheriff by telephone, but he cannot understand them and tells them to see him personally. But they decline and proceed to find his Under-sheriff and are admitted to the store. The main property cannot be found, they demand admission to the safe, and no one has the combination. Locksmiths are procured and they batter away at the vault all night. In the meantime the Sheriff appears and forbids them and requests them to wait with a guard on the property until daybreak, when the combination can be procured. In the morning the Sheriff again appears with counsel and endeavors to persuade them to desist and wait for the combination. Finally the boy appears but the combination has been changed and will not work. For fifty long and weary hours the work progresses before the iron doors finally yield to the heavy blows of the workman's hammer. At last they give away and what property is found is taken. The Sheriff bonds it back and all are now enjoying the luxury of a lawsuit.

SOME OF THE QUESTIONS TO SETTLE.

Were the executions in the Sheriff's hands valid? Was he in lawful possession of the building? Was he bound to have the key to see his goods while stored, or the combination to a safe, or vault, or bank where he deposits things in the custody of the law for safe keeping? Was the replevin process valid? Was the pretended demand by telephone authorized by law? Did the Sheriff refuse to give up the property? Were the papers made out in New York in advance of a demand and refused in due form of law? Can an innocent man's property be destroyed to get the goods without a demand and refusal from him to remove the obstruction? Can several parties in New York city assign accounts to one of their number and allow him to swear he owns the goods represented by the same? Such are the great complications in the affairs of Sheriff's duties. The courts alone can unravel them with the aid of good counsel.

THE BLACK MARIA.

Another much needed and humane improvement introduced by Sheriff Wheeler is the employment of the jail ambulance, called the Black Maria, for the conveyance of prisoners. Prior to its use, prisoners were dragged through the streets in irons and frequently in chained gangs. Sometimes black and white, male and female boys and girls, the hardened in crime and the beginner, all mixed and mingled together. Some tattered and battered, some half clad, some in rags, some intoxicated and loathsome in appearance. The moral effect was degrading and disgraceful. Often the people along the route begged to have them taken some other way, where their children would not be exposed to the degrading influence. The sight was obnoxious, loathsome and most repulsive. What is there more disgusting to every sense of decency than to see a blue coated officer of the law club in hand, dragging a drunken man or woman through our streets, foul with bad whisky and fouler tongue? These things were, but are no longer tolerated. The expense is no more than it was before. It is simply a question of who should be credited with the statutory fee, the police or the Sheriff. The system itself is right and proper. If the people tolerate these crimes from the abuse of liquor, they should not thrust the degraded presence of their victims in the face of decency and innocence. The tender feelings of little children should be guarded with zealous care. Another humane institution is the patrol wagon of the city and for the same reasons. Decency belongs to all things. It is to be regretted that these things are made necessary, but such being the fact, let's keep the infamous from the innocent as much as possible. Bad men sometimes creep into all trades, and more especially the saloon business. By their conduct in abusing their license they are bringing the whole system into disrepute. Aye, they are undermining the very pillars upon which rested the foundation of our free government. They seek to continue their existence through their political power. They bid defiance to law and order This is despotism, and in time will destroy them. There is a constantly growing sentiment among the people, created by the crimes committed, and the appeals of the suffering victims in hospital and jail that will in time sweep the whole traffic from the earth. Despotism always defeats itself. Civil liberty respects the rights of every American citizen alike. The people will not see it abused; it cost too much to rescue it from the despotic emperors of Europe. To those who trifle within its sacred precincts we say, beware. Obey the law and respect this sacred institution. If bad men are allowed to trample down the statutes, our safety, our protection is gone. The dignity of the law must be maintained to render life, property and liberty secure. Without the enforcement of law there can be no liberty but the liberty of the brute. Might will triumph over right when well enforced laws do not prevail. In an enlightened land like this, men should obey the golden precept of the Divine teacher, "Do unto others as ye would have them do unto you." If all truly felt this sentiment in their very hearts, Sheriffs would be little needed. Men would do nothing to degrade their fellow men, but all would unite in raising them up and making them better. But, as it is, an officer is needed to enforce the law, for in the present condition of things eternal vigilance alone is the price of liberty.

CONCLUSION.

In these short sketches, made in the first instance for our own personal use, we have simply cited some of the most celebrated cases as they occurred under each administration. Our time and space was limited to a few columns per week. Some day we may again take up the pen in our leisure moments and try and sketch other things of historical value. Oneida county has a brilliant historical record, and is continually growing in population, influence and power. While in the towns many farms are being consolidated, in the large villages, and cities of Utica and Rome new and varied industries are constantly springing up with a call for more skilled men and laborers. Under these circumstances it is very essential that its highest executive officer should be a competent and exemplary man. In the beginning we spoke of the origin and duties of the Sheriff's office. As the President rules the nation, and the Governor rules the State, the Sheriff rules the county. That is he is its highest executive officer. The officers of the law, the military and even the entire power of the people are subject to his command. Many times the duties are onerous and thankless. He has to act in conformity with complicated laws and every state of facts changes the condition of things. Hence he must be a man of sound judgment, discretion and thought. He cannot succeed himself, but must complete all the business of his term. All thing must be done fairly and without fraud, deceit or oppression. If he violates any trust, he is liable to the injured party. He must do no wrong, but always do right under severe penalties. A conviction for any offense forfeits the office. The Governor may remove for cause, and appoint a successor until the next general election. He can hold no other office. His bonds are $10,000 with a renewal of $10,000 more for each and every year in office, besides these he must give military bonds, and bonds for the extraordinary proceedings. We might comment for hours on these duties and qualifications, but for the purposes of these sketches it is unnecessary. On the whole, Oneida County has been governed by good Sheriffs. Most of them are gone and are now unknown, save as their acts appear on the old and fast fading books and records.

Some of these may be used as precedents for others to follow, and some serve only as light houses, warning their successors which way to go to avoid their errors. Such is the experience of life.

While writing these sketches we have received many kind words of commendation from old residents who are now living over the days of their youth. Some have written and others have called at our office.

HON. GEORGE GRAHAM.

Among them may be mentioned our old and venerable friend, Hon. George Graham of Oriskany. He is probably the oldest Deputy Sheriff in the shire. He has lived through the varied scenes and experiences of nearly four score years of the 18th century. Yet his step is firm and his mind is clear and bright as ever. In our researches we have frequently found his name away back on the old court records as Deputy Sheriff, Grand Juror and Justice for the General Sessions. He was General Deputy under Col. David Moulton during the great McLeod trial, and had charge of the military patrol and independent battery mounted to defend the jail and Court House against the marauding bands of Canadian patriots. Whitestown at this time, was fortified and well guarded. He was Captain of the Guard. An armed force was encamped near by to rescue the prisoner from the civil authorities. These were foreigners from Canadian soil. Officers of the United States were on hand to await their movements, and the military on the frontier was all out under the command of Maj. Gen. Scott. They were ready to march on Canada at a moment's notice, if England violated the rules governing such cases. Those were exciting times for Oneida county. Since those days, our esteemed friend has held many other positions of public trust. He was Supervisor for Whitestown many years and has been Member of Assembly and Sergeant at Arms of the State Senate. For years he was the companion and agreeable associate of Judge Pomeroy Jones, the historian of Oneida county. They sat together on the county Board of Excise for several terms and often conversed about the annals and early incidents of this once wild and almost pathless wildness.

If we shall ever again take up the pen and search the records of our shire, we shall be pleased to relate some of the incidents and anecdotes remembered by the venerable and gifted Deputy Sheriff. But for the present, we must conclude our sketches and consign them to the archives of the Oneida County Historical Society We fully realize that they have been like the records of all historical events, mingled with sorrow and gladness. Such is life.

"There are smiles in the morning and tears at
   night,
   The wide world over.
There are hopes in the morning and prayers at
   night
   For many a rover.
There are tears unwept and songs unsung,
   And human anguish keen;
And hopes and fears and smiles and tears,
   But the blessings fall between.

◁FINIS.▷

www.ingramcontent.com/pod-product-compliance
Lightning Source LLC
Chambersburg PA
CBHW022204020726
47496CB00008B/2874